MANDIE
AND THE
DANGEROUS
IMPOSTERS

Mandie Mysteries

1. *Mandie and the Secret Tunnel*
2. *Mandie and the Cherokee Legend*
3. *Mandie and the Ghost Bandits*
4. *Mandie and the Forbidden Attic*
5. *Mandie and the Trunk's Secret*
6. *Mandie and the Medicine Man*
7. *Mandie and the Charleston Phantom*
8. *Mandie and the Abandoned Mine*
9. *Mandie and the Hidden Treasure*
10. *Mandie and the Mysterious Bells*
11. *Mandie and the Holiday Surprise*
12. *Mandie and the Washington Nightmare*
13. *Mandie and the Midnight Journey*
14. *Mandie and the Shipboard Mystery*
15. *Mandie and the Foreign Spies*
16. *Mandie and the Silent Catacombs*
17. *Mandie and the Singing Chalet*
18. *Mandie and the Jumping Juniper*
19. *Mandie and the Mysterious Fisherman*
20. *Mandie and the Windmill's Message*
21. *Mandie and the Fiery Rescue*
22. *Mandie and the Angel's Secret*
23. *Mandie and the Dangerous Imposters*

———

Mandie's Cookbook

MANDIE
AND THE
DANGEROUS
IMPOSTERS

BETHANY HOUSE PUBLISHERS
MINNEAPOLIS, MINNESOTA 55438

Mandie and the Dangerous Imposters
Lois Gladys Leppard

All scripture quotations are taken from the
King James Version of the Bible.

Library of Congress Catalog Card Number 93–74539

ISBN 1–55661–459–4

Published by Bethany House Publishers
A Ministry of Bethany Fellowship, Inc.
11300 Hampshire Avenue South
Minneapolis, Minnesota 55438

Printed in the United States of America

In Memory of
Mrs. Vesta Guffey Davidson,
who designed Mandie's apron and bonnet.*

(August 11, 1905–October 15, 1993)

Gone from sight, but not from my heart.

*The apron and bonnet patterns are available in *Mandie's Cookbook*, published by Bethany House Publishers.

About the Author

LOIS GLADYS LEPPARD has been a Federal Civil Service employee in various countries around the world. She makes her home in South Carolina.

The stories of her own mother's childhood are the basis for many of the incidents incorporated in this series.

Contents

"What time I am afraid, I will trust in thee."

Psalm 56:3

Chapter 1 / Where Is Tsa'ni?

Mandie Shaw was up and dressed by the time the rooster crowed in the backyard. There was something she *had* to do. Before she left with Uncle Ned. She would be staying at his house for only a few days, then she would return home to prepare for going away to school. But she *had* to do this now and she dreaded doing it.

Slowly opening the door to the hallway, the small thirteen-year-old girl whispered to herself, "Please, God, don't let anyone see me."

After carefully looking around outside her room, she slipped into the dark corridor and hurried silently down the staircase to the front hall. She quickly slid back the bolt on the front door, quietly pushed it open, and stepped outside onto the front porch.

"I have to do this," she told herself, taking a deep breath and rushing down the long walkway to the gate in the white fence along the road. There she paused with her hand on the latch and gazed across the way to the churchyard with its many, many tombstones.

"Here I go," she muttered, flipping back the latch and pushing the gate open. She ran as fast as she could to the cemetery gate. She flung it open and hurried to a fresh mound of dirt with a new stone marking the grave. The year 1901 was engraved across the stone.

Mandie felt her knees grow weak and she sank to the ground. Tears came into her blue eyes as she cried with a trembling voice, "I really and truly did love you. I did." Her breath caught in her throat and she paused to swallow. "Oh, how I wish you could know. I really and truly did love you. So much . . . much more than I ever realized until I lost you."

Mandie sat back on her heels and wiped her eyes with the corner of the frilly white apron that covered her blue gingham dress. "I have to go now. Uncle Ned will be looking for me." She glanced back across the road. She saw that Uncle Ned had brought his wagon from the back of the house into the driveway. He stepped down and started toward the front door. "Goodbye, my darling. I have to go."

Uncle Ned looked in her direction and saw her coming out of the churchyard. He waited at the porch steps for her.

Mandie lifted her long skirts and ran to him. She called to him in a still-shaky voice, "Here I am, Uncle Ned. I'm coming."

The old Cherokee Indian came to meet her halfway up the walkway. He looked down into her face and silently put his arm around her small shoulders.

"Uncle Ned, I—I had—to tell him goodbye,"

Mandie said as she fought back fresh tears. "I really did love him . . . so much."

"I know, Papoose," Uncle Ned said, tightening his hug. "But we must go to eat now. Then we go."

They went into the house, and when they entered the dining room, Mandie saw that all the visiting relatives were sitting at the table. Her grandmother, Mrs. Taft, her mother, Elizabeth, and her Uncle John were also seated at the large table. She hurried to her mother's side.

"Mother, how did you get down here? You're too weak from the fever to be doing this. Maybe I'd better stay home and take care of you," Mandie said as she clasped her mother's hand.

"Amanda, I didn't walk down those stairs from my room. Your Uncle John carried me. I thought I'd feel better if I could sit at a proper table for a proper meal for a change. I'm so tired of being sick," her mother explained with a smile. She gave Mandie's hand a tight squeeze.

Mandie smiled back and said, "I'm so happy that you are able to sit at the table, Mother."

Uncle John, sitting beside Elizabeth, looked at Mandie and told her, "Don't worry about your mother, Amanda. I'll see that she's taken good care of."

"Oh, Uncle John, I'm so glad you married my mother after I—I lost—my father," Mandie said, slipping into a chair next to Elizabeth. "You're like a second father to me. And I love you both so much." She glanced down the long table and realized everyone was listening. With a big smile she said, "And I love you all, too. I'm so glad you're all my kinpeople. As soon as we eat, I am going home with Uncle Ned to visit my Cherokee kinpeople who live near him. He's not really my uncle, you know. In fact, he's not even kin to me, except that he was my father's best friend, and now he's my best friend.''

Everyone smiled and the room echoed their murmurs of love.

"We'd better eat, Amanda," her mother told her. "Uncle Ned wants to get on the road."

"Yes, ma'am," Mandie said. She looked over at Uncle John.

"Let's return thanks," Uncle John said as he glanced around the table. Everyone bowed their heads and he gave thanks for the food and for Elizabeth's recovery from the fever.

Mandie softly added her own thanks. She was so grateful to God for sparing her mother.

Aunt Lou, Uncle John's huge Negro housekeeper, entered the room with two platters of hot food, which she placed on the table. Liza, the young maid, came along behind her with hot biscuits. And Jenny, the cook, brought in a steaming coffeepot. She set it on the sideboard and began filling the cups that were sitting there. With all the extra company it took all three of the servants to wait on the table.

As Mandie ate, she kept watching Uncle Ned's plate so she would know when he was ready to leave. Uncle Ned excused himself from the table just as she swallowed her last bite of food.

"You may go now too, dear," Elizabeth told her. "Give my love to Sallie and your great-uncle Wirt and all the others. And, Amanda, please don't get involved in any dangerous adventures while you're there. One of these days you may get in trouble with all this chasing after mysteries that you do. Remember that now."

"Yes, ma'am, I'll remember what you said," Mandie assured her as she stood up. "And, Mother, don't you do anything that you shouldn't. I want you to hurry and get well."

Elizabeth laughed and said, "I will remember what you said also, dear."

Mandie rushed around the table to plant a kiss on her grandmother's cheek. "Will you be here when I get back, Grandmother?" she asked.

"No, dear, I must get home to Asheville and see about Hilda now that your mother is recuperating. We've been gone so long already," Mrs. Taft reminded her. She put an arm around Mandie's waist and drew her close. "I'll see you in Asheville when you return to school. You behave yourself now while you're visiting Uncle Ned and his family."

"I will, Grandmother, and I'll see you soon," Mandie said. Then with a wave around the room she rushed through the doorway into the kitchen to tell Aunt Lou, Liza, and Jenny goodbye. The three women were waiting for her with big smiles, and even Jenny's husband, Abraham, who was Uncle John's gardener, was there to say goodbye. Snowball, Mandie's white cat, was busy devouring food from a saucer under the cook table.

Mandie hugged Aunt Lou. The big woman admonished her as she drew Mandie into her arms. "And you be sho' you don't git in no trouble, you heah. And don't you worry none 'bout yo' mama, now. She not only got us, she also got Mistuh John to take care of huh."

"You hurry back now, Missy 'Manda," Liza told her when Mandie turned to hug her.

Jenny picked up a picnic basket from the table and said, "Heah, Missy, we done packed lunch fo' you and de Injun man."

Mandie took the basket as she gave Jenny a squeeze and said, "Thank you, Jenny, I'm sure it's something real good."

"It sho' is," Abraham told her. "Sumpin' *really* special."

Mandie put an arm around the old man's shoulders and said, "If you say it's something special, I know it must be. Thank y'all, every one of you."

Uncle Ned opened the door to the hallway behind her and looked into the kitchen as he said, "Must go now, Papoose."

"I'm ready now, Uncle Ned," Mandie said as she picked up Snowball and started out the door. Looking back into the room, she blew a kiss to her friends and said, "I love you all. Bye."

The servants all smiled and returned the expression of love.

"I have to get my bag, Uncle Ned," Mandie told him as they entered the hallway. She handed him the picnic basket to hold, and said, "I'll be right back."

"I help Papoose," Uncle Ned offered.

"No, Uncle Ned. I'm not taking much because I won't be staying long at your house," she called back to him as she hurried toward the staircase. "I'll meet you at the wagon."

In her room, Mandie picked up Snowball's red collar and leash from a nearby chair and fastened it onto him. Then she grabbed her bonnet from the bureau and tied it on over her long blond hair. The blue gingham of the bonnet and dress matched her blue eyes.

"Let's go, Snowball," she told her cat as she scooped him up in one arm and picked up her valise sitting nearby with her other hand. She hurried to join Uncle Ned in the yard.

As the horses pulled the wagon out onto the road, the sun just cleared the horizon and moved into the deep blue sky. The cool North Carolina mountain air was invigorating.

They traveled out of town and then through the woods. Birds chirped in the trees, and now and then a squirrel ran across their path. Mandie had tied Snowball in the back of the wagon, but he had enough slack in his leash to jump occasionally in a fruitless effort to catch butterflies fluttering by.

Mandie was happy and she hummed now and then. She squirmed in her seat beside the old Indian, and Uncle Ned glanced at her and smiled.

"I just can't wait to see Sallie and tell her about my trip to Europe with Grandmother and Celia," Mandie remarked.

"Papoose have to wait. Long journey to Deep Creek by wagon," Uncle Ned told her.

"We should have ridden horses, Uncle Ned. That way we could take short cuts and get there faster," Mandie replied, looking up at him.

"Too steep, too dangerous for Papoose on horse," Uncle Ned said.

"Well, at least we have the good food Jenny packed for us," Mandie remarked as she glanced toward the back of the wagon at the picnic basket sitting next to Uncle Ned's bow and arrows.

They rode on up the rough road and finally stopped by a spring bubbling out of the rocky side of the steep mountain. Uncle Ned pulled the wagon off the narrow road and tied the horses.

"I'm glad you stopped, because I'm positively, absolutely starving to death," Mandie said with a big giggle as she jumped down from the wagon.

Uncle Ned smiled at her as he reached for the picnic basket. Mandie pulled a quilt out of the back of the wagon and spread it on the ground as a tablecloth, then she picked up Snowball and tied him to a bush nearby.

"No running away on this big mountain, Snowball," she warned her white cat. He looked up at her and protested loudly. Mandie continued, "Now if you'll behave yourself, I'll give you something to eat."

She helped Uncle Ned unpack the basket and was delighted to find fried chicken, biscuits, a jug of tea, some apples, and, of all things, a whole chocolate cake that Jenny had made for them. Mandie squealed with delight. "Look, Uncle Ned, we've got a whole cake—a chocolate one at that—all by ourselves!"

Uncle Ned sat down on the edge of the quilt and smiled at her. "We not save Sallie some cake?" he asked.

"Oh, of course, Uncle Ned. We couldn't possibly eat this huge cake all by ourselves," Mandie replied as she dug deeper in the basket and came up with some fried fatback, which she knew was meant for Snowball.

She laid the fatback on the grass by her cat and said, "And, Snowball, you've got a special treat, too." He sniffed and began eating, moving from one side to the other in his excitement.

Mandie and Uncle Ned were almost finished with their meal when the old Indian suddenly spoke in a soft voice, "Do not move, Papoose!" Mandie quickly looked at him and saw that he was looking up, over Mandie's head. She felt danger and held her breath as Uncle Ned slowly moved around to the other side of the wagon, where he carefully retrieved his bow and arrows.

Mandie glanced at Snowball and saw the fur on his back rise. He growled and tried to jump free from his leash. At that same moment, an arrow from Uncle Ned's bow flew through the air and struck its target with a dull thud. A huge black panther gave a piercing cry and came tumbling down from a tree limb over Mandie's head.

Mandie snatched up Snowball and rushed backward quoting her favorite Bible verse under her breath, "What time I am afraid I will put my trust in Thee." The panther hit the ground right in front of her, but she discovered that Snowball's leash stopped them from going very far. She knew only God could save her.

Uncle Ned ran around the beast and put himself between it and Mandie and Snowball. He shot another arrow, and the panther flopped motionless to the ground this time.

"Papoose, get in wagon," the old Indian told her as he quickly snatched up the remnants of their food and stashed it in the picnic basket. He grabbed the quilt and tossed it into the wagon with the basket.

Mandie, with her legs feeling weak, managed to jerk Snowball's leash free from the bush she had tied it to and climbed into the wagon. She squeezed the cat so hard he complained loudly and wriggled to get loose. Uncle Ned jumped into the wagon, grabbed the reins and, with a low whistle to the horses, got the vehicles rolling.

"Whew! That was close!" Mandie said, blowing out a relieved breath as she clung to the seat with one hand. "But, Uncle Ned, why the hurry to leave? You killed that panther, didn't you?"

"Yes, Papoose, but may be mate nearby. Another sound in trees up there," he explained as he continued urging the horses on.

"Oh, goodness, I never would have thought of that," Mandie said with a gasp. "Uncle Ned, I'm so glad you promised my father that you would look after me when he . . . when he left this world."

Uncle Ned reached to squeeze Mandie's hand where it rested on the seat. "I keep promise," he said. "Jim Shaw good man."

Mandie looked at him with a big smile. She loved Uncle Ned.

They traveled the rest of the day without any more incidents, and just as the sun began slipping behind the trees, Mandie spotted the Cherokees' farmland ahead. She could smell supper cooking, and as they came around a sharp bend in the road, a group of log cabins came into view.

"We're here, Uncle Ned. We're at your house at last!" Mandie cried excitedly.

Uncle Ned smiled and slowed the wagon to turn in beside the largest cabin in the group. Mandie had been here before and she glanced around at the familiar buildings. The house was similar to the one in which Mandie had lived with her father before he died. It was made of logs chinked together with mud, and a huge rock chimney stood at one end. Horses grazed behind a split-rail fence near the barn at the rear of the house.

Then Mandie saw Sallie, Uncle Ned's granddaughter, standing in the open doorway of the house. She came running out to greet them as Uncle Ned brought the wagon to a halt.

"Oh, Sallie, I'm so glad to see you," Mandie said, excitedly jumping down from the wagon as she held on to Snowball.

Sallie, wearing a long, full skirt with a ruffled blouse and multicolored beads around her slender neck, embraced Mandie. "It is good to see you, too," she said. Her black eyes sparkled with excitement.

Uncle Ned took the wagon into the backyard as the girls walked to the front door of the cabin.

"My grandmother has supper ready," Sallie told Mandie.

"How did she know what time we would get here?" Mandie asked.

"You forget. The Cherokees have their own line of communication from one mountain to another," Sallie said with a smile.

"Oh, yes, of course," said Mandie. "I knew that. They pass the word from one brave to another along the way. But you know, we didn't see a single brave on our way here."

"That is because the braves did not wish you to see them," Sallie explained, "but they saw you."

Morning Star, Uncle Ned's wife, met them at the door and embraced Mandie. In her limited English she said, "Love . . . Wash . . . Eat."

"Morning Star, you are learning more English. That's wonderful," Mandie said, and she gave the old woman a big hug.

The woman motioned toward the wash basin sitting on a shelf nearby and then toward the kettles of food hanging in the huge rock fireplace. The long table was already set with dishes.

At the far end of the room were several beds built into the wall and covered with corn-shuck mattresses. Hanging curtains could be pulled around each one. A spinning wheel and a loom sat in a corner. A ladder leaned against the wall, and Mandie knew she and Sallie would climb it to the room above when it came time to sleep.

Mandie quickly set Snowball down, removed his leash, and hung it on a hook by the door. Then she went to wash her face and hands. She dipped water into the wash pan on the shelf from a large bucket sitting nearby, washed her face and hands, and then dried herself with a clean towel hanging on a nail.

"Whatever you've cooked smells delicious!" Mandie told Morning Star as Uncle Ned came in the back door.

Morning Star just smiled at her, not understanding much of what she said.

Uncle Ned washed, then motioned for Mandie and Sallie to be seated at the table. Morning Star took their bowls to the kettles over the fire, filled them with food, and brought them back to the table. Then she brought cups of hot sassafras tea from another kettle.

Mandie glanced at her bowl and was relieved to see it held corn chowder. Morning Star had cooked owl stew when she was here before, and Mandie had had to force herself to eat it.* After Morning Star was seated, Uncle Ned returned thanks.

Mandie was awfully hungry, so when Sallie passed Mandie the bread, she took a large slice. Soon she had eaten every bite of the bread and every spoonful of the chowder. Morning Star,

---

*See the note at the bottom of p. 176.

watching her, quickly took the bowl, hurried to the kettle, and refilled it.

"Eat," the old woman told Mandie as she placed the bowl back in front of her.

"Thanks, Morning Star. I was about half starved to death," she said with a laugh.

"Eat good," Uncle Ned told her with a big smile while Morning Star replenished his bowl.

"I am anxious to hear about the journey you made to Europe with your grandmother and your friend Celia," Sallie told Mandie.

"I have lots and lots to tell you, and as soon as we finish eating, I will begin," Mandie said. "But tell me, what does Tsa'ni want to see me about?"

Sallie shrugged and said, "He told me to send you word that he wanted to see you, but I have not seen him since then."

"He must be around somewhere," Mandie said.

"No one knows where he has gone," Sallie replied. "When we got the message that you were on the way, I looked for him everywhere but could not find him. No one had seen him."

Mandie sat thinking for a moment and then said, "He's probably up to something—as usual."

"One never knows what he will do next," Sallie agreed.

"Well, he's not going to fool me with all his tales this time," Mandie declared.

She could never believe anything he said. He didn't like her because she was only one-fourth Cherokee and he was full-blooded. He considered her white, and declared all white people his enemies.

"He is not trustworthy," Sallie agreed.

"He probably thinks I came all the way up here

just because he wanted to see me about something, but I really and truly came because I wanted to see you, Sallie. We've so much catching up to do," Mandie said.

"Yes, you are right," Sallie said. "And I am glad that you came to see me."

"If Tsa'ni wants to see me, he'll have to find me. I'm not going looking for him," Mandie declared.

That's what Mandie was saying, but all the time she was wondering how she could find him. She just had to know what he wanted to see her about.

Chapter 2 / Mysterious Men in the Mountain

Mandie and Sallie talked for half the night. Snowball curled up on the foot of the bed and went to sleep. As they lay in bed, Mandie told Sallie about her adventures in Europe, and Sallie told Mandie about the schoolhouse that had been built for the Cherokees since Mandie's last visit.

"The schoolhouse is finished?" Mandie asked, sitting up in surprise.

"The missionary Riley O'Neal has it almost completed. Everyone has been helping," Sallie replied as she leaned up on her elbow to look at Mandie.

"But I wanted to help with it," Mandie said with a disappointed sigh. "I told Mr. O'Neal I would."

"But we could not wait for you to come back from Europe, Mandie," Sallie said. "It will soon be time for school to start and the schoolhouse must be ready."

"Yes, I understand," Mandie said. "I suppose I can't be a part of everything. Could we go see it tomorrow?"

"I am sure we could. I have been going over there as often as I can," Sallie said. "You might like to know Tsa'ni is still not agreeable to having the schoolhouse built."

"Oh, goodness," Mandie said. "Has he caused any trouble? I remember the way he acted at the council meeting when the Cherokees voted to allow Mr. O'Neal to build the schoolhouse. He didn't want anyone to learn white people's ways, and especially not from Riley O'Neal, who is from up north."

"He still talks that way, but I do not know of any trouble he has caused," Sallie replied.

"Do Tsa'ni's parents, Jessan and Meli, not know where he is?" Mandie asked.

"No, they do not, but they are used to him disappearing every once in a while. His grandfather, your uncle Wirt Pindar, has not seen him either. I asked him today," Sallie explained.

"I'd like to visit my uncle Wirt and aunt Saphronia while I'm here. My mother sends them her love," Mandie said as she sank back down onto her pillow.

Sallie, still on her elbow, looked at Mandie and said with a smile, "Someone else has been asking about you."

Mandie, now getting sleepy, asked, "Who?"

"Dimar," Sallie said.

Mandie rose up again and said, "Really? I'd like to see Dimar. Do you think he'll come here to your house while I'm visiting you?"

Dimar Walkingstick lived in the mountains above Deep Creek. Mandie and her friends had met him when they had been lost in the woods. He was a tall, handsome Cherokee boy, two years older than Mandie.

"I am sure he will. He has been coming here to go with me when I work at the schoolhouse," Sallie explained.

Mandie pondered Sallie's reply for a moment. Maybe Dimar liked Sallie. At one time he had seemed interested in Mandie.

"Hmmm, I'm sleepy," Mandie said as she lay back down. "We'd better go to sleep or we won't want to get up in the morning."

"That is true," Sallie said as she lay back on her pillow. "I hope you have pleasant dreams."

"You too, Sallie, good-night," Mandie murmured as she turned to face the wall. Snowball meowed, got up, walked around in a circle, then lay back down at Mandie's feet.

Mandie couldn't go to sleep right away. She wanted to do some private thinking. So much had happened while she was gone to Europe. She greatly appreciated the journey with her grandmother and Celia, and she knew she would not have met Jonathan if she had not gone. She smiled when she remembered he had promised to come to see her and Celia someday.

But she felt disappointed that she had not been here to help with the schoolhouse. Anything concerning the Cherokees was always important to her. Her father's mother had been a full-blooded Cherokee, and Mandie had dearly loved her father who had passed away in April of the year before.

She could still close her eyes and see her father

putting up a split-rail fence around their property at Charley Gap. His red curly hair was always mussed up, and his bright blue eyes always twinkled when he looked at her. He had not inherited his mother's Cherokee features or coloring.

Mandie felt a pain in her heart as she remembered his death and then his funeral and his grave on top of the mountain above Charley Gap. She and her father had been isolated from all their relatives, and Mandie had not even known she was one-fourth Cherokee until after his death.

Mandie quietly cleared her throat as she lay there in the upstairs room in Uncle Ned's house. She would never get to sleep if she didn't change her thoughts. Maybe if she just thought about places she could look for Tsa'ni she would finally go to sleep.

This worked, and she drifted off in slumber.

She was dreaming of her father when suddenly she realized Sallie was shaking her awake.

"Mandie, it is time to get up," Sallie told her. "I smell the coffee cooking."

Mandie opened her eyes, yawned, and sat up in bed. She looked out the window across the room. Either it was cloudy or it wasn't daylight yet.

"Sallie, what time is it?" she asked as she swung off the bed. Snowball, displaced by Mandie's action, jumped off the bed and began washing his face.

Sallie laughed and said, "It is time to get up."

Mandie smiled at her and walked over to look out the window. "I believe it's cloudy," she remarked.

Sallie joined her and said, "Yes, it is cloudy, but it is later than the sky looks. The roosters have already crowed, and I hear my grandmother in the kitchen downstairs." She turned away to get her clothes.

"Then we'd better get dressed," Mandie said, reaching for a dress. She had hung her clothes on the nails in the wall of the upstairs room.

She happened to glance out the window again just in time to see a flash of white clothing. Someone darted through the trees across the road. "Sallie, there's someone in the woods over there."

Sallie came to join her. "I see nobody over there, Mandie," she said, frowning as she looked outside.

Mandie kept watching the woods, but nobody appeared and nothing moved. "I know I saw someone run through the woods," she said, turning away from the window. She put on her dress and stooped to find her shoes.

"Probably some brave on his way for early fishing or hunting," Sallie said as she finished dressing.

"Probably," Mandie agreed as she slipped her shoes on and buttoned them. Straightening up, she shook out her long skirts and looked at Sallie. "You don't suppose that could have been Tsa'ni I saw over there?"

"I think if it had been Tsa'ni he would have stopped to watch our house to see if you were up yet. Remember, everyone knows you are here now," Sallie said as she opened the door. "I am ready to go downstairs." She waited for Mandie to join her.

Mandie snatched up Snowball and followed Sallie down the ladder to the room below. Morning Star was busy cooking, and the smell of coffee made Mandie suddenly hungry.

"Good morning, Morning Star," Mandie greeted the old woman with a smile. She set Snowball down, and he began roaming the room.

Morning Star looked at her and with a big smile, she replied, "Morning, good, yes."

"You are getting better and better at understanding English, Morning Star," Mandie told her as she reached to squeeze the woman's hand.

Morning Star squeezed back before she walked over and put the food on the table. "Eat," she said to the girls.

Mandie looked around the room. "Where is Uncle Ned?" she asked.

Sallie asked her grandmother in Cherokee and then told Mandie what Morning Star said: "My grandfather has already had his breakfast and has gone to get a horse shoed."

The girls sat down, and Morning Star joined them at the table. Mandie was glad to see she had prepared eggs and bean bread, and there were pomegranate preserves to finish things off.

Snowball rubbed against Mandie's ankles under the table, and Morning Star got up and went to a shelf near the fireplace. She brought back a plate of scraps she'd saved for Snowball and put it under the table. The cat quickly devoured it.

"Sallie, would you like to go looking for Tsa'ni?" Mandie asked as she passed a bowl of eggs across to her friend.

Sallie looked at her in surprise and said, "Why would you want to go looking for Tsa'ni?"

"Well, I suppose I'm just curious about his wanting to see me," Mandie replied with a little smile. "You know how it is. If a mystery pops up, I just have to solve it."

Sallie laughed. "Yes, that I know," she agreed. "But as you said before, one cannot always believe everything that Tsa'ni says. He likes attention, and I suppose that is why he does naughty things."

"One time he *really* was in trouble, remember? Of course it was due to his own making, but we did rescue him," Mandie reminded her. "I'd hate to think he needed help again and we didn't try to find him."

Sallie's smile got bigger this time. "All right, I will go with you to look for him," she said. "But, no one has seen him, so I do not know where to begin."

"In the woods across the road," Mandie suggested. "I *know* I saw someone over there."

"If he was walking in the woods over there, then he does not need our help," Sallie said. "I will ask my grandmother if she has seen anyone in the woods this morning." She turned quickly to Morning Star and spoke in Cherokee.

Morning Star looked from Sallie to Mandie and with a big smile began rapidly speaking. Sallie answered her in Cherokee and then translated for Mandie. "My grandmother has not seen Tsa'ni and has not seen anyone in the woods. She says we should go see his parents, Jessan and Meli, and if they do not know where he is, then we should go see his grandfather, your uncle Wirt Pindar, in Birdtown."

"Let's try his parents first, right after we see the school," Mandie said as she finished her food. And then she suddenly realized she didn't know where the school was. "Where did they build the school, Sallie?" she asked.

"The schoolhouse is a little piece beyond the hospital from here," Sallie said as she, too, ate the last of her food. "They built it far enough away from the hospital so the school children will not make noise to disturb anyone staying in the hospital."

"I'm anxious to see it," Mandie said as Morning Star stood up. "Will you tell your grandmother where we are going?"

Mandie rose from the table as Sallie did. After Sallie had explained to her grandmother where they were going, Morning Star looked at both girls and said firmly. "Back . . . Eat."

"We'll be back to eat, Morning Star. Thank you," Mandie told the woman as they went out the front door. Snowball quickly followed his mistress into the yard.

"Are you going to allow Snowball to come with us?" Sallie asked as she looked down at the cat.

Mandie stopped for a moment. "I suppose so," she said. "I don't think I need to put his leash on in a place like this."

At that moment the girls heard a horse coming up the road. They turned to see who it was.

"Why, it's Dimar!" Mandie said excitedly as the horse and rider turned into Uncle Ned's driveway.

"Good morning," Dimar called to the girls, slipping down from his horse and throwing the reins around a nearby post. He came toward them smiling.

"Good morning, Dimar," Mandie said, looking up at him as he came closer. "I do believe you've grown a foot since I was here last time."

"No, not that much, but quite a lot," Dimar said, smiling. "I heard you were coming to visit, so I came down from the mountain. Where are you girls going?"

Sallie glanced at Mandie and waited for her to answer.

"We were going to see the new school and look

for Tsa'ni," Mandie said. "He sent me a message that he wanted to see me, and now that I'm here he's nowhere to be found."

Dimar frowned and said, "He is around somewhere. He likes to be secretive."

"But I asked everyone—his parents, his grandfather—and no one has seen him," Sallie said as the three stood there in the yard.

"I am sure we can find him," Dimar said.

"You mean you'll help us look?" Mandie asked.

"Yes, I will help you look," Dimar promised.

"I wanted to see the new schoolhouse, too. Sallie says it's almost finished and I didn't get to help," Mandie said.

"Yes, Sallie and I have been helping. I will go with you to see it," Dimar said. "You girls must be careful. There are strange men on the mountain."

Mandie perked up at once. "Strange men on the mountain?" she queried.

"Yes, no one knows who they are, and they seem to be trying to dig up the whole mountain," Dimar said with a worried look on his handsome face.

"The whole mountain?" Mandie asked with a loud gasp.

"Yes, they are moving from one place to another on the mountain and digging everywhere they go," Dimar explained.

"Are they Cherokee?" Sallie asked.

"No, they are white men and they do not live anywhere around here," Dimar said. "That is what makes it so strange. There have been no white people living on the mountain."

"Let's go see them," Mandie said.

Dimar looked at her and said, "We can go look

at them, but I would not want them to see us, because we do not know who they are."

"Well, is anyone trying to find out who they are and what they're doing?" Mandie asked.

"I do not know of anyone who has talked to them," Dimar said.

"You mean the Cherokees are just going to let them dig up the whole mountain and not do anything about it?" Mandie asked in surprise.

"No, the men will not be allowed to dig up the whole mountain. We are watching them first, then we will ask them questions," the Indian boy explained.

"Let's go watch them. Maybe we can figure out what they're doing," Mandie suggested.

Sallie looked at her and said, "Mandie, we do not know where these men are from and we do not know who they are."

"I know, but we could look for them and for Tsa'ni, too," Mandie said impatiently. "Let's go by the schoolhouse first. I'd like to see it."

"Yes, we will do that," Sallie agreed.

"I must put my horse inside the fence until I return," Dimar said, picking up the reins. "Then we will go." He led the horse through the gate and into the backyard, took off the saddle, threw it across the fence, and then came back to join the girls.

"We will go the shortcut," Dimar told the girls as they walked onto the road. He pointed to the woods on the other side. "There is a path in there." He led the way. Snowball came racing after them.

"I thought I saw someone wearing white clothes dash through the woods this morning when we got up," Mandie remarked. "It wasn't you, was it, Dimar?"

"No, I was at home until I came here on my horse. It was probably someone out for an early walk," the boy replied. "Now we cross the creek over here, and then the path straightens out."

The girls followed Dimar to the creek. Dimar held out his hand to help Mandie cross the creek, but she picked up Snowball and held him with one arm and caught up the hem of her long skirts with the other. She jumped across the creek and landed on a large rock on the opposite shore. Her feet skidded for a moment, but she quickly regained her balance. Snowball got free and scrambled into the weeds.

Sallie watched, then chose a different place to jump across where she would land on sand.

Dimar watched the girls and then followed them. "I see you girls do not need my help," he said with a laugh. Leading the way along a narrow path, he said, "We will soon arrive at the hospital, and then the schoolhouse will be beyond."

As they walked single file down the trail, they had to push tree branches back out of their way now and then. The path became narrower, so Mandie picked up Snowball and carried him. Then they came to a dense part of the woods and the pathway completely disappeared.

"Do not worry," Dimar reassured them as they looked around in wonder at the end of the trail. "I know the way through the trees. It is not very hard to get through, and it is much nearer than going down the road."

"I'll have to trust you, Dimar, because I've never been through here before," Mandie said. "When the hospital was built, we all rode down there in wagons or on horses along the road."

Suddenly Mandie heard something fly through the leaves of a nearby tree, and Dimar abruptly stepped back. He pushed the girls to the ground. Mandie held tightly to Snowball.

"Stay down," he ordered in a loud whisper. "Someone shot an arrow." He stooped down beside them and put a hand on both girl's shoulders.

Mandie and Sallie lay flat on the mossy ground. Mandie tried to rise, but Dimar kept a firm grasp on her shoulder.

"It's just someone shooting arrows—probably hunting, or practicing, or something like that," Mandie protested in a loud whisper.

"You and Sallie stay here. I will see who it is. Do not follow me. Stay here." He was firm about his orders as he rose and moved slowly forward through the trees.

Mandie whispered to Sallie, "I'm going to see what's going on." She got up and began moving forward in a stooped position. She held tightly to Snowball, who was trying to get free.

"No, Mandie, stay here," Sallie protested. But when Mandie paid no attention to her, Sallie slowly followed.

Mandie had lost sight of Dimar and she couldn't hear a thing. She started to straighten up. Maybe whoever had been there was gone by now. Suddenly another arrow whizzed by right in front of her. She dropped to the ground, but she got a glimpse of someone wearing white clothing. The underbrush was too thick to see who it was.

Mandie got up and started forward again.

Sallie gasped behind her, "Mandie, stop!"

Mandie looked back and shook her head. She put her finger across her lips to warn Sallie to be quiet. Then she slowly continued ahead in a stooped position. Suddenly she bumped into a pair of legs and, with her heart beating wildly, she looked up.

It was Dimar. Mandie relaxed and Snowball finally escaped his mistress's arms. He jumped around in the weeds.

"Oh, Dimar, you scared me," Mandie exclaimed in a low voice.

"I told you girls to stay put," Dimar said. "There was someone ahead of us, but they have run away now. I couldn't tell who it was." He sounded disappointed.

"I saw someone wearing white clothes through the bushes, but I couldn't tell who it was either," Mandie said. She turned to Sallie behind her and asked, "Did you see someone?"

"No, I did not. I was watching where I was going," Sallie replied. She stood up to join Mandie and Dimar.

"Let us continue on our way," Dimar told the girls. "Please stay close behind me." Mandie looked around to make sure Snowball was right behind them.

They followed Dimar through the trees until another path appeared. This one was wide enough for the three of them to walk side by side.

Soon they came to the Cherokee hospital. Mandie stopped to stare at the white frame structure. Two simple columns held up the roof over a small front porch. She had not been back here since she helped in the ceremony to open the hospital.

Dimar and Sallie paused at her side.

"Is there anyone in the hospital right now? Has it been used yet?" she asked her friends. She picked up her white cat, who was now rubbing around her legs.

"No one has used it. Dr. Woodard still comes to the house of anyone who needs him when he is in this territory," Sallie explained. "Mostly, my grandmother prepares herbs and poultices for the sick."

"You mean the Cherokees aren't going to use the hospital?" Mandie asked.

"Oh, yes, they will. They just have not done so yet," Dimar said.

The three walked on.

"Do y'all walk all the way to the schoolhouse when you're helping with work there?" Mandie asked.

"No, we ride our horses or take my grandmother's cart," Sallie explained.

Just as they passed the hospital building, Mandie turned to look at Dimar and saw something flash by the edge of her vision. She thought it was someone in white clothes again, but she wasn't sure this time. She stopped to gaze around the road.

"Why are you stopping again?" Dimar asked as he and Sallie paused in the road.

"I thought I saw someone in the trees over there," Mandie said, pointing to their right. "But I'm not sure."

"Should we look around?" Dimar asked.

"Oh, no, let's go on. I'm beginning to think it's probably Tsa'ni following us around," Mandie said with a sigh.

They continued down the road toward the schoolhouse. Mandie kept alert after that, but when she saw the schoolhouse, she became excited and forgot all about someone in white clothes.

She set Snowball down, and he immediately ran to the front door of the schoolhouse.

Chapter 3 / Caught Snooping

The schoolhouse was constructed of hand-hewn logs with a huge rock chimney rising in the center of the roof. The building stood two feet off the ground on rock pillars, with room for storage underneath. Hanging at the end of the full-length front porch was a large iron bell. The front door was in the center with a glass window on either side protected by wooden shutters which were now open.

"Oh, I love it!" Mandie said, clapping her hands as she, Sallie, and Dimar paused to admire the front. "It looks like it could be someone's house."

"It is," Dimar told her. "The missionary Riley O'Neal has a room at the back in which he lives. The front part is the schoolroom."

"He lives here?" Mandie said in surprise. "Well, I suppose he has to have somewhere to live, and living right here is awfully convenient for him. Is he at home now, do you know?"

"He may be," Sallie replied. "I think he is still doing some work inside."

"We could go inside and look for him," Dimar said, leading the way.

He pushed open the door to the schoolroom and Mandie stepped into a large room with log benches and rough tables set about. A rock chimney had been built into the far wall and a huge heater was vented through it.

"Isn't he going to have any desks?" Mandie asked as Sallie and Dimar followed her into the room. Snowball stayed outside.

"Yes, he has them ordered from up north, but they have not arrived in time for the start of this school year, so the Cherokee men have made these benches and tables to use until they get here," Sallie explained.

Mandie paused by a large chalkboard on the wall. "At least he did get this in time." She inspected the chalk and brushes lying on the tray in front of the board.

"Yes, this board was donated by a school near Asheville. They were replacing it with a much larger one. The missionary heard about it, so he and Jessan, father of Tsa'ni, and Dimar went to get it and brought it across the mountain," Sallie explained.

"This door goes into the missionary's room," Dimar said, pointing to a door near the chalkboard. "Shall we knock and see if he is there?"

"Yes, do," Mandie said.

Dimar knocked on the door. It was not shut tightly so it swung open at his touch. The three glanced into the room beyond. No one was there. Mandie saw a bed built into a corner of the room and a small table and several stools, all made of hand-hewn logs. A shelf ran the entire length of the room. On this were stacked books and papers.

As she walked near the fireplace, which was the other side of the chimney, she noticed a cast-iron cookstove with the stovepipe going through the wall opposite the chimney.

"He has his own stove to cook on," she remarked to her friends. "I wonder if *he* knows how to cook, being he's from up north and so educated and everything."

Sallie laughed, "No, he does not know how to cook. He would like for my grandmother to teach him."

"You would have to interpret for them," Mandie said. "But do you think he would eat food like the Cherokees cook?"

"Maybe, but my mother has knowledge of cooking for white people and she will be helping him, too," Dimar said with a huge smile.

"I'd like to see his results," Mandie said with a laugh that was cut short as she glanced back at the open door.

"That you shall see, then," a tall, red-haired man said in a loud voice as he strode into the room. He walked right up to Mandie, looked down at her with a big smile, and put his hand out in greeting. "It's good to have you here again, Amanda," he said. "I'm honored that you've come to visit me."

Mandie was flustered at being caught in Mr. O'Neal's private quarters. "I apologize for being here. You see, when we knocked on your door it just came open and . . . we just . . . walked in," she told the missionary. She noticed he wasn't wearing the black suit he had worn when she met him earlier in the summer. Today his attire was a homespun white shirt and light-tan trousers. He was carrying a light-tan, wide-brimmed hat.

"You are all welcome anytime," Riley O'Neal replied, still smiling as he glanced at Sallie and Dimar. "Please feel free to come visit whenever you like. And as soon as we get the cookstove going, you will all have to come back and try my food. You see, I only know how to cook like we do up north. I'm going to learn the way you cook down here because I want to be part of everything."

"Then you must teach us how to cook northern style," Sallie said with a smile.

"That I will do as soon as I get supplies in to cook," he said. Turning back to Mandie, he asked, "And what do you think of the new schoolhouse?"

"Oh, it's so nice. I'm sorry I wasn't here to help build it," Mandie replied as she walked to the doorway and looked out into the schoolroom. "Is there anything left to do that I might be able to help out on? I'll be staying at Uncle Ned's house for a few days."

They all stepped into the schoolroom and looked around.

Sallie spoke up, "We need to make curtains for the windows. I already made measurements. Some of the women have made green cushions for the benches and there is enough material left for the curtains."

"I'd like to help," Mandie said.

"The balance of the material is at my grandfather's house. The cushions are at Dimar's house waiting for the first day of school," Sallie explained. "We could begin the curtains when we return."

"That's good. I'm glad I can help a little," Mandie said.

"You will be asked to do more than make curtains," Dimar said with a sly grin. He looked up at Mr. O'Neal.

The missionary explained, "Yes, we were going to ask you to help Sallie with the little children the first day of school, if you're still here."

"Do what?" Mandie asked in surprise.

"We think the first day of school will be quite confusing for the younger children who have never attended such a place," the missionary said. "We have asked Sallie to help keep them quiet and still. That way they'll be off to a good start and will understand that they have to behave and listen in order to learn when they come in here."

"I'll be glad to help Sallie," Mandie said, and turning to her Indian friend, she asked, "But do these children understand English?"

"Some do and some do not," Sallie replied. "We will speak both languages to them. This will encourage them to learn English."

"And I will help with the older boys who do not know English," Dimar said.

Mandie suddenly remembered that they had started out to look for Tsa'ni. They had to be back at Uncle Ned's house for their noon meal, so there wasn't much time.

She asked the missionary, "Have you seen Tsa'ni today? We are looking for him because he had sent word that he wanted to see me, but no one knows where he is."

"No, in fact I haven't seen him in several days," Riley O'Neal said. "Since I'm living here now and I've been so busy trying to get everything finished, I don't see much of anyone unless they come here."

"If you do see him, would you please tell him

that I'm looking for him?'' Mandie asked as she walked toward the front door.

"Yes, I will,'' Riley O'Neal replied.

They all stepped out the front door, and Mandie saw the missionary's wagon with his horse still hitched to it standing by the road.

"I have been to Bryson City depot to get the books that came in on the train,'' the missionary told them as he walked to the wagon and pulled the tarp back. The bed of the wagon was full of boxes and bags.

"Then we will help you unload them,'' Dimar said, reaching to pick up a carton.

"Thanks. If you will just set them in the school-room, I'll unpack and organize everything,'' Mr. O'Neal said as he also lifted a box and followed Dimar back to the schoolroom.

Mandie and Sallie climbed up into the wagon and looked around for something light enough for them to carry.

"I'll take this bag,'' Mandie said, stretching the drawstring to look inside the burlap bag. "Oh, what do you know? It's groceries.'' She smiled.

Sallie also found a lightweight bag that she could take inside. Then, as the two fellows took more book cartons from the wagon, the girls found two valises with tags on them showing a Boston address.

"Probably his clothes,'' Sallie remarked as they took them into the schoolroom.

When everything had been transferred to the plank floor of the schoolroom, the young people offered to help the missionary unpack the cartons.

"That would be a big help, thank you,'' Riley O'Neal said as he glanced around the room. "I think we need to sort the books into stacks and place them in a row beneath the blackboard. That way they will be ready to distribute to the students when they arrive the first day of school.''

They unpacked the boxes, and Mandie noticed there were books for all the basic subjects—reading, writing, and arithmetic—just like Mr. O'Neal had told the Cherokee council there would be. The Cherokee people had voted earlier that summer on whether or not to allow the missionary to build a school for their children. Tsa'ni had cast the only dissenting vote. He had said the Cherokees did not need to learn ''white people's ways.''

Mandie bent down to place an armful of books in one stack when Mr. O'Neal stooped at the same time and said, ''I'm certainly glad I didn't have to pick you up off the road this time.''

She knew he was referring to the first time she had met him. She had been out on a lonely mountain road when she slid down a hill and landed in front of his wagon.

A frown crossed her brow as she said emphatically, ''*That* was an accident.'' She stood up and straightened her long skirts. ''What about pencils and paper. Do you have any?''

''Yes, thanks to my students back home. They've sent boxes of paper and pencils,'' he explained as he rose to his feet.

''Well, then—'' Mandie began.

Mr. O'Neal looked at her and interrupted, ''Amanda, I'm sorry about what happened back home with you, the fever, and—''

Mandie quickly stepped away from him and said, ''I don't want to talk about it.''

Dimar finished emptying the last carton and

stood up. "I think we have to go now if we are going to look for Tsa'ni," he said, glancing at Mandie.

"Yes, and we were going to look for the strange men digging up the mountain," Sallie added.

Mr. O'Neal followed Mandie across the room to her friends. "Have you seen the men who are doing the digging?" he asked.

Sallie and Dimar shook their heads as Sallie replied, "No, but we are looking for them because Mandie wanted to see them."

"Have you seen them?" Mandie asked the missionary.

"No, but I've been hearing about them," said Mr. O'Neal. "If you happen to see them, I'd like to hear about it."

"We will let you know if we do," Dimar promised.

The missionary followed the three outside. "I thank you all for the help you've given me with the books," he told them.

"You are welcome," Mandie said without even glancing his way, and she urged her friends on. "We'd better hurry," she said. She snatched up Snowball from the yard and started walking down the road.

Sallie and Dimar waved to the missionary and followed her.

As soon as they were out of sight of the schoolhouse, Sallie asked Mandie, "Do you not like the missionary?"

Mandie sighed, then said, "Oh, he's all right. He just wanted to talk about something that I didn't want to discuss." As she spoke she realized none of her Cherokee friends had even mentioned what had happened back home earlier. She knew they all understood her feelings.

Sallie turned to Dimar and asked, "Are we going up the mountain in the hopes of seeing those men digging?"

"Yes, we will go this way," he replied as he veered to the right across a field and the girls followed.

"Don't forget to watch for Tsa'ni on the way," Mandie reminded her friends.

They climbed steep hills and pushed their way through thick underbrush. Once in a while they would stop to listen. Only the birds and an occasional squirrel disturbed the silence. Mandie carried Snowball so he couldn't run away.

When they finally reached the top of the mountain, they stopped to rest. Mandie could clearly see familiar landmarks miles away. The three gazed in every direction at the landscape below, searching for the strange men.

"I see a wagon down there on that winding road," Dimar remarked, squinting to see better. "I cannot see who is in it, but it looks like an ordinary Cherokee wagon."

The girls looked in the direction he pointed.

"Yes, it is just an ordinary wagon," Sallie agreed.

Mandie glanced at it and then turned to look down in the opposite direction. "I see some Cherokee men walking along a path over there," she commented as Snowball squirmed to get down.

Dimar and Sallie followed her gaze.

"Yes, you are right," Dimar agreed.

"Which direction are those strange men supposed to be?" Mandie asked.

"No special place. They have been seen in various locations digging as hard as they could dig," Dimar replied.

"Who has actually seen them?" Mandie asked.

"Tsa'ni was the person who started this story about the strange men digging up the mountain. Some of his friends have seen them, but I have not seen them and I do not know who else has seen them," Dimar explained.

"Then it's possible Tsa'ni is making all this up," Mandie declared.

"I do not think that is true, because his grandfather, your uncle Wirt, believes him even though most of the time his grandfather does not have faith in Tsa'ni's sayings," Dimar replied.

"Then we should go see his grandfather," Sallie said. "But that we cannot do right now because we must return home to eat."

"Maybe Uncle Ned will be back home by the time we get there and we can ask him about the strange men," Mandie decided.

"Yes," Sallie agreed.

Dimar led the way back down the mountain and on to Uncle Ned's house. Mandie kept a tight hold on Snowball. She knew if he got away from her on the mountain she might never find him.

As they came within sight of Uncle Ned's, Mandie was delighted to see the old man's wagon in the yard. He was back, and Mandie was sure he always knew everything about everything. Although he had been at Mandie's house in Franklin and had escorted Mandie to his house just the day before, he had been away from his farm this morning and would have had a chance to learn about the strange men.

Morning Star had food ready and had set the table by the time the young people came in through the front door. But they saw no sign of Mandie's uncle.

"Where is Uncle Ned?" Mandie asked, looking around the cabin.

Sallie asked her grandmother in Cherokee and then told her friends, "My grandfather is getting wood from the barn for the fireplace."

"Then I must help," Dimar said, rushing out the back door.

Mandie set Snowball down and followed Sallie to the wash basin to clean up. The food smelled delicious, and she suddenly realized how hungry she was. The country air always gave her an appetite.

Uncle Ned came in with his arms full of chopped wood, and Dimar was behind him with another load. They stacked the wood by the fireplace and then went to wash.

"Sit," Morning Star told everyone, and they found places at the table. The old Indian woman carried bowls to the kettle in the fireplace and brought them back, filled with a delicious-smelling soup.

"What is it?" Mandie asked Sallie as she looked at the steaming bowl placed in front of her.

"Soup made from the chowder we had last night, with a piece of ham to flavor it," Sallie explained.

Mandie was delighted to know it was something she dearly loved. She watched as Morning Star placed plates of freshly made bread before them. Finally the woman sat down at the table.

Uncle Ned gave thanks to the Big God, and everyone started eating and talking.

"Uncle Ned, have you heard about these strange white men who are supposed to be digging up the mountain?" Mandie asked him across the table.

"I heard," Uncle Ned replied. "I see. East Ridge."

"You saw them?" Mandie asked excitedly. "Who are they? What are they doing?"

Sallie and Dimar leaned toward Ned to hear better.

"Do not know," Uncle Ned replied, and he sipped his coffee. "Two white men dig here, dig there, dig everywhere."

"Did you talk to them?" Mandie asked.

"No, no, Papoose, not let them see me," Uncle Ned told her. "Must wait. See what they do."

"Oh, shucks!" Mandie said disappointedly.

"What did they look like?" Dimar asked.

"One big, one little," Uncle Ned replied as he helped himself to the bread. "White shirts, tan trousers, big hats hid faces."

"What did they dig for, my grandfather?" Sallie asked Uncle Ned.

He smiled at Sallie and said, "My granddaughter, we not know. We watch. We wait."

"Uncle Ned, have you seen Tsa'ni today?" Mandie asked as she hastily ate her soup.

"No, Papoose, not see Tsa'ni today," the old Indian told her with a big smile. "Tsa'ni nowhere today."

"You know he wanted to see me, but I haven't been able to find him," Mandie explained. "Maybe we could find the strange men and ask what they're up to. And Tsa'ni might be watching them too."

"No, Papoose, not talk to strange men. Stay

away from strange men," Uncle Ned said. "This Cherokee business for Cherokee men. Papoose not to go to strange men. That firm." He looked sternly at Mandie.

"All right, Uncle Ned. I won't go find the strange men and talk to them," Mandie promised. "But what if the strange men find me?"

"Strange men not be looking for Papoose!" Uncle Ned said emphatically. "Papoose go somewhere else, not near men."

"We did go to the schoolhouse this morning," Mandie told him. "It looks nice. I believe Riley O'Neal will have a good school going for the Cherokees."

"Yes, he has boxes and boxes of books, my grandfather," Sallie said. "We helped him unpack them. And Mandie and I will be making the curtains for the schoolhouse while she is here."

"Then Papoose must do that. Not be here long," Uncle Ned reminded Mandie.

"I will, Uncle Ned. That won't take long," Mandie said, as she finished her soup. She turned to Morning Star and smiled as she said, "Soup is good, Morning Star. Real good."

Mandie was sure the old woman understood her, because she, too, smiled and said, "Good. Good."

Mandie looked at Dimar and Sallie and asked, "Do y'all want to go look for Tsa'ni this afternoon? When we come back we could work on the curtains, Sallie."

"I can go with you for a while, then I must go home and work," Dimar said.

"Yes, I will go too, and then we will cut out the curtains," Sallie agreed.

Mandie looked back at Uncle Ned, who had just

finished his soup, and asked, "Do you want to come with us?"

"No, Papoose, things to do," he said. As he and Morning Star rose from the table, he looked at Mandie and said, "Not stay gone long now."

"We won't," Mandie promised as she and her friends stood up.

Morning Star set a plate of scraps under the table for Snowball, who gulped it all down.

"Are we taking Snowball this time?" Sallie asked.

Mandie sighed and said, "I suppose I'll have to let him come along, since I don't have anywhere to put him while I'm gone."

As they left, Mandie was secretly hoping they'd run in to the strange men somewhere on their search for Tsa'ni.

Chapter 4 / Where Is Uncle Wirt?

As soon as the three young people stepped out into the yard, Mandie stopped her friends to ask, "Why don't we go see Uncle Wirt first? He might have heard from Tsa'ni. And, Dimar, you said he believed the story about the strange men, so we could tell him that Uncle Ned said he saw the strange men too."

"Mandie, we would need a cart or wagon or something to go all the way to Bird-town to see your uncle Wirt and come back this afternoon," Dimar explained.

Mandie turned to Sallie and asked, "Does your grandfather have something we could borrow to ride in?"

"We have a small cart that my grandmother uses," Sallie said. "My grandfather always uses his wagon. I could ask my grandmother for use of the cart. We need to tell her where we are going anyway, if we are going that far."

"The cart would be all right," Dimar said.

51

"Please ask her, Sallie," Mandie told her. "We'll wait right here for you." Snowball chased a chipmunk nearby.

Sallie went back inside the house. While Mandie waited with Dimar, he smiled at her and said, "I am glad you have come back to visit. I would like to hear all about your journey to Europe. I hope to go there myself someday."

"Oh, you'd really enjoy it, Dimar," Mandie said excitedly. "We had mysteries almost everywhere we went, besides all the sightseeing we did. And, you probably have heard, my grandmother brought this orphaned Irish girl back with us. Her parents died a long time ago and her mother's best friend had given her a home. But while we were there, the woman had an accident that made her permanently incapable of taking care of Mollie anymore."

"That was very good of your grandmother to do that," Dimar said.

"Well, my grandmother only brought Mollie back with us because Mollie has an aunt somewhere in the United States," Mandie explained. "But the authorities in Ireland didn't know where. So when my grandmother finds the aunt, Mollie will go live with her. And in the meantime, Mollie went home with my friend Celia Hamilton, who lives in Virginia, you know, because that was the last place the aunt had been heard from."

"How many countries did you visit?" Dimar asked as he leaned against the rail of the fence.

"Oh, goodness, let's see. We went to London, England—that was first—then on to Paris, France; Italy; Germany; then to Belgium; Holland; and Ireland," Mandie recounted. "Then we had to come home. We didn't go to Scotland and Wales as we had planned." Her voice became sad and she dropped her gaze as she remembered the reason why they had returned home.

"Before you go back home please take time to tell me all about these places. I would greatly enjoy hearing about these countries. I have never known anyone before who has been to Europe," Dimar said.

"I promise to take the time to tell you and, believe me, it will take some time to go back over the adventures we had," Mandie said. "I'll only be here a few days because I have to get back home in time to prepare for school. I'll be going back to the school in Asheville this year."

"I have an idea and would like to ask your permission," Dimar said, suddenly smiling. "I know there are many Cherokee people who would like to hear what you want to tell about your journey. Would it be possible to get them all together someplace and hear what you have to say?"

Mandie blushed as she glanced at Dimar and then looked across the yard. "I don't know whether other people would want to hear about what we did or not. Besides, most of our Cherokee people don't understand English," she said.

"That is no problem. I could translate, and I am sure Sallie would help. Please, this would be something interesting to our people. And we get very little knowledge outside our own circle," Dimar said.

"Well, if you insist," Mandie said reluctantly. "But I insist that this will be real informal-like. Maybe we could sit outside somewhere around a fire at night or something."

"That is a very good idea," Dimar said with a smile. "Provided it doesn't rain on us. In that case, would you think of doing this in the schoolhouse? It is a very large room, you know, and would hold a lot of people."

"All right. You fix it all up—Oh, here comes Sallie," Mandie said, looking toward Uncle Ned's house.

Sallie came up to them and said, "Dimar, my grandmother says it will be all right if you want to harness up the cart for us to use. But that we must hurry, because she expects us back before suppertime."

Dimar started walking toward the barn. "That's fine. I'll get it ready."

In a few minutes, Dimar was driving the cart with one girl on either side of him on the seat. Snowball sat in the back.

Dimar told Sallie about his plans to give the Cherokee people the opportunity to hear about Mandie's journey to Europe.

"Oh, that is a wonderful idea!" she exclaimed. "That was so thoughtful of you to think of that. Our people will be so grateful."

"They may not approve of everything I did on that trip," Mandie said with a laugh. "So I think I'd better skip some of it, like eavesdropping on Rupert in Germany, and Jonathan and Celia and me getting lost in the catacombs in Italy. It all sounds to dumb to tell now."

Dimar glanced at Mandie and said, "Will you tell me about all the left-out details later?"

"Oh, sure, Dimar," Mandie said.

Dimar drove fast, taking shortcuts on barely passable trails and they were soon at Bird-town. Mandie had been here before, but as she gazed around the locale, she reminded herself that this was part of the Cherokee Indian reservation, the original land where her Indian ancestors had lived.

The wide, dirt road ran through rows of log

cabins which were separated by small fields of crops. Dimar pulled into the yard of the largest house in the group. This was the home of Mandie's great uncle, Wirt Pindar.

Mandie jumped down and hurried to the doorway, where her great aunt Saphronia, Wirt's wife, stood to welcome them. She was a tiny Indian woman, and she seemed to have a million wrinkles in her tan face.

The old woman grasped Mandie in her arms, exclaiming, "Jim Shaw's papoose! Love, Papoose!"

Tears came into Mandie's blue eyes at the mention of her father, and she tightly hugged the little woman. "I love you, Aunt Saphronia."

Sallie picked up Snowball, then she and Dimar joined Mandie at the door. When everyone had entered the house, Aunt Saphronia insisted on serving hot coffee, which was already brewed and hanging in a black iron kettle over the open fire.

"Coffee, then we talk," the woman insisted as she motioned the young people to sit at the table. Snowball explored the room.

Aunt Saphronia filled four cups with coffee and brought them to the table, where she sat down with them.

"Now we talk," the old woman said with a big smile as she reached to pat Mandie's small, white hand.

"Where is Uncle Wirt?" Mandie asked, sipping the hot coffee.

"He gone to see Jessan," Aunt Saphronia replied, taking a huge sip of the steaming coffee.

"To Tsa'ni's father's house?" Mandie asked. She looked at her friends and added, "I suppose we should have gone by there first, since they live near Uncle Ned.''

"When will he return home?" Dimar asked the woman.

"Late, late—maybe dark," Aunt Saphronia said.

The three young people exchanged glances.

"When was the last time you saw Tsa'ni, Aunt Saphronia?" Mandie asked.

"Been days," she said. "Not visit us much."

Mandie decided to try another subject. "Have you heard about the strange men who have been seen digging in the mountain?"

Aunt Saphronia immediately looked at her and, as she shook her head, said, "Bad men. Cherokee land. Cherokee people not like."

The three young people looked at each other, and Dimar asked, "Have you seen them?"

"No, no, not see. Hear," the woman replied, shaking her head again. "Wirt say bad men in mountain, digging up Cherokee land."

"Do you know if Uncle Wirt has seen them?" Mandie asked.

"No, no, Tsa'ni tell Wirt. He see," Aunt Saphronia replied. "Wirt not see."

The three young people finally finished their coffee and decided to leave. Mandie picked up Snowball in her arms and promised to visit Aunt Saphronia again before she went back home.

Dimar rushed the cart through the narrow, bumpy trails again. At one point Mandie thought she saw someone in the trees, someone wearing white.

"Look!" she cried out to her friends as she pointed to the place she thought someone had appeared.

Dimar and Sallie quickly looked, both asked, "What?"

"Oh, shucks, they're gone now," she said as Dimar urged the pony on with the cart. I think I saw someone in the trees back there—and they were wearing white."

"Too late now," Dimar said.

"We do not have time to stop and investigate if you are planning to visit Tsa'ni's house in hopes of finding Tsa'ni or your uncle Wirt," Sallie reminded her.

"You're right," Mandie said. "It's strange I keep seeing someone dressed in white, and they seem to be following us around."

"You forget," Dimar said. "All the Cherokees walk through the woods now and then and lots of our people wear white, especially the women."

"I know," Mandie acknowledged. "I hope we'll at least catch Uncle Wirt at Tsa'ni's house before he goes home."

But when they arrived at Tsa'ni's house and knocked on the door, no one was home except Tsa'ni's mother, Meli. She understood very little English, and Sallie and Dimar had to tell her what they had come for.

"She says she has not seen Tsa'ni for days," Dimar told Mandie.

"And your uncle Wirt has not been here today," Sallie added. "Tsa'ni's father, Jessan, has been helping build a house for a family in the valley on the other side of the mountain and will not return until late tonight."

"Oh, shucks!" Mandie said, and let out a big sigh. "We've been disappointed every way we turn today."

"Yes, and now I must return this cart and pony,

and get my horse," Dimar told her. "I have work to do at my home."

"And we have curtains to make, Mandie," Sallie reminded her.

"Yes, and we might as well begin," Mandie agreed.

They returned to Uncle Ned's house. When Sallie explained to her grandmother where they had been, Morning Star told the three young people that Uncle Ned was also working with Jessan on the house in the valley.

As Snowball curled up in front of the fire and went to sleep, Mandie and her friends sat down. Mandie said, "I wonder if we could just begin all over again in the morning."

Dimar rose and said, "Yes, I will come back down early in the morning. Sallie, ask your grandfather what time Jessan will be going back to work on that house, and we will speak to him before he leaves."

"Yes, I will do that," Sallie promised. "But you must get here early. I know my grandfather leaves early when he has things to do."

"I will be waiting in the yard before the rooster crows tomorrow morning," Dimar promised, giving Mandie a big smile as he went out the front door.

Sallie spoke in Cherokee to her grandmother, who was sitting by the fire.

Then she turned to Mandie and said, "I just told my grandmother we are going upstairs to begin work on the curtains for the schoolhouse. Come on."

Mandie followed Sallie up the ladder to the other room next to Sallie's. A large roll of green cotton material lay on the bed. Sallie picked up a basket sitting on the floor and took out pins and a pair of scissors. She pulled out a rolled-up piece of paper and stretched it out on the bed.

"This is a drawing of what the curtains will look like and what size they must be," she told Mandie. She took a ruler from the basket and explained, "We can just unroll the cloth, measure it, and stick pins in it where we need to cut."

"Oh, yes, that should be easy enough," Mandie agreed as both girls knelt by the bed and began straightening out the green cloth.

With Mandie's help, Sallie soon had the material cut into pieces and they began pinning up the hems.

"Where do you suppose Uncle Wirt is?" Mandie asked as they worked on the curtains. "Tsa'ni's mother had not seen him. But maybe Aunt Saphronia didn't know *where* he was to see Jessan."

"Perhaps he was with my grandfather working on that house," Sallie suggested.

"But don't you think he would have gone by to see Tsa'ni's father on his way to work on the house? Remember, Aunt Saphronia said he was gone to Tsa'ni's house," Mandie said, pausing to look at her friend.

Sallie sat back on her heels and thought for a moment. "That is a puzzle. We need to ask my grandfather about it."

"I'd like to ask your grandfather some more questions about those strange men, since he said he saw them," Mandie said, reaching for a pin.

Sallie reminded her, "He warned us not to go looking for those strange men, Mandie." Sallie folded a neat hem and pinned it.

"I know," Mandie said. "I just want to ask him if he has been there again and, if so, were they wearing white."

Sallie stopped to look at her. "You still believe

you keep seeing someone wearing white, do you not?" she asked.

"Yes, I know I have been seeing someone wearing white. Now it might have been that each time it was just one of our people walking through the woods or whatever, like Dimar said. But someone shot arrows across our path, remember? And I know you and Dimar saw that happen," Mandie said.

"Yes, but again that might have been someone practicing or shooting at a squirrel," Sallie said. "They might not have been trying to shoot at us."

"But, Sallie, they would have heard us coming through the woods. We were talking and not trying to be quiet about it," Mandie said. "I am sure they saw us."

"We must tell all this to my grandfather," Sallie said. "He can help us think."

"Think," Mandie repeated the word. Uncle Ned was always telling her to think first, then act. And she rarely remembered to do things in that order. "Yes, I suppose I'll have to do a lot of thinking about this, too."

When Morning Star called up the ladder to tell them their supper was ready, the girls had already done a lot of work on the curtains. Mandie rose and rubbed her knees. She was sore from kneeling so long.

"I'm not used to all this hard work," she joked.

"But it is not *hard* work. It is *pleasurable* work," Sallie told her with a smile. "I enjoy sewing things. Maybe I will be a seamstress when I am older—that is, if I can learn to do a good job."

"Then you will have to come home with me sometime and let Aunt Lou teach you. She is an excellent seamstress," Mandie said.

"Yes, I would like to do that," Sallie agreed.

The girls went down the ladder to supper. Uncle Ned was back and Snowball was awake and was roaming the room in search of food.

Morning Star had cooked a ham, baked potatoes, and made a big pan of cornbread. There was also a pot of peas. When the old woman began putting the food on the table, Mandie could hardly wait to begin eating. Everything smelled delicious.

Uncle Ned returned thanks and they began the meal.

"Uncle Ned, have you seen Uncle Wirt today?" Mandie asked.

Uncle Ned, sitting across the table, looked at her and said, "No, not see Wirt today."

"We went to his house today and Aunt Saphronia said he had come over here to Deep Creek to Jessan's house. We went there and Meli said she had not seen him, but that Jessan had been gone all day working on the house in the valley," Mandie explained between bites of ham.

"Yes, Jessan be with me, work on house. Not see Wirt," the old man said with a thoughtful frown. "I take Jessan home. Wirt not there."

"Well, I suppose he went somewhere else," Mandie said. "Have you seen those strange men anymore?"

Uncle Ned looked sharply at her. "No," he said. "Why Papoose ask?"

Mandie could almost read the old man's mind. She knew he was thinking she had been out looking for the men. "Well, I just wanted to know what they were wearing. You see, I keep seeing someone in the woods that I know is wearing white, but I never can see who it is. Then at one place, when we were going through the woods with Dimar to the schoolhouse, someone shot arrows right in front of us, but we never did see who it was."

"Arrows? At you, Papoose, you, my granddaughter, and Dimar?" Uncle Ned asked with a big frown on his old, wrinkled face. "Where this happen?"

Mandie looked at Sallie and asked, "Can you explain where we were? You know the countryside around here better than I do."

Sallie explained to her grandfather where they had been walking when this happened.

"I check on this," Uncle Ned said. "See if arrow still there. Papoose must be careful. My granddaughter must be careful too."

"Do you have any idea about who it might have been?" Mandie asked.

"No Cherokee shoot at another Cherokee," Uncle Ned said firmly. "Must be stranger."

"You mean the strangers digging up the mountain?" Mandie asked.

Uncle Ned looked at her for a moment, and then said, "Maybe. Strange men may be dangerous."

Mandie drew a deep breath and said, "Uncle Ned, somebody has got to find out who those men are and what they are doing."

"Papoose not do this. Cherokee men do this," the old man said.

At that moment, someone entered the house, and Mandie turned to see who had come in. She was surprised to see Jessan standing at the doorway.

"Come, eat," Uncle Ned told him.

"Not eat. Look for my father," Jessan said. "Been here?" He spoke to Morning Star in Cherokee.

"No," Uncle Ned said as Morning Star shook her head. The old man talked rapidly to Morning Star.

She replied in Cherokee, "Not see Wirt today."

Uncle Ned said, "Morning Star not see him."

"Aunt Saphronia told us Uncle Wirt had gone to visit you, but when we got to your house, Meli said she had not seen him," Mandie said quickly.

"That is why I look for my father," Jessan said. He turned to leave. "I must go to Bird-town and see if my father home now."

Uncle Ned rose from the table and said, "Wait, I go with you."

"No, not necessary," Jessan said. "I go."

"I help," Uncle Ned insisted as he walked toward Jessan.

"Eat," Jessan told the old man.

"I finish," Uncle Ned said. "Drink coffee when we come back. Hurry. Dark soon."

"I take my horse. Faster," Jessan said as the old man joined him at the door.

"I take my horse also," Uncle Ned agreed.

As they left the house, Mandie looked at Sallie and said, "Uncle Ned seemed to be worried about Uncle Wirt, like he thought something must have happened to him."

"Your uncle Wirt is an old man. He could be sick or hurt somewhere," Sallie explained.

"I hope not," Mandie said, laying down her fork.

Morning Star spoke up, "Eat." Then she spoke rapidly in Cherokee to Sallie.

Sallie translated for Mandie: "She wants us to hurry and finish so she can go sit with Meli until Jessan and my grandfather get back," she explained.

"I'll hurry, then," Mandie said, picking up her fork. "Sallie, tell your grandmother to go ahead when she finishes, and we can clear the table."

"Yes, we can," Sallie agreed, and repeated

Mandie's offer in Cherokee to her grandmother.

Morning Star quickly swallowed the last bite from her plate, smiled at the girls, and stood up. She walked over to the corner and took a black shawl from a peg. Then she threw it around her shoulders, smiled again, and went out the door.

As soon as they were finished, Mandie and Sallie made quick work of the table. Mandie fed Snowball a plate of scraps by the fireplace. Sallie went up the ladder and brought down the curtains they had been working on.

"I brought everything so we can work by the fire until everyone gets back," Sallie said. "This table is much better to work on anyway."

"Yes, we don't have to kneel down," Mandie said with a laugh as she rubbed her still-sore knees.

"They won't be gone long because it won't take them long on horseback," Sallie said as they began threading needles.

Then a thought occurred to Mandie and she asked Sallie, "Don't you think it's strange that Tsa'ni has not been seen for days, and now his grandfather suddenly disappears?"

Sallie looked at her thoughtfully and said, "I suppose it does look strange, but I do not see how the two are connected."

"I just hope they find Uncle Wirt," Mandie said.

Mandie had an uneasy feeling about the two disappearances. There seemed to be some mysterious things going on.

Chapter 5 / Sitting in Wait

Mandie and Sallie worked fast on the green curtains as they discussed the day's events. Time flew. Snowball chased threads for a while and then curled up on the hearth by the fire to go to sleep.

"Will you be happy to return to your school in Asheville?" Sallie asked.

"I suppose so," Mandie said. "It's a lot different from the country school I went to at Charley Gap. So are the students. A girl named April Snow keeps things lively with her tricks, but she doesn't get away with anything. And I love Miss Hope, but Miss Prudence is a little stiff."

"And will you be seeing Thomas Patton from the boys' school there in that town?" Sallie asked as she tucked in a hem and sewed it down.

Mandie smiled as she thought of Tommy Patton. He was the son of one of her mother's school friends, and her family had visited them at their home in Charleston, South Carolina.

"He'll make a nice, rich husband for some girl someday," Mandie said.

"You have so many friends your age, but there are very few people my age around here. In fact, my grandfather says if the Cherokee people do not start having more children, our race will die out," Sallie told her.

Mandie looked at her and said, "Then you must marry a Cherokee man when you grow up, and you must have a dozen children." She laughed at the expression on Sallie's face.

"I would never marry anyone unless I deeply loved him," Sallie said. "I am not sure I would ever want to marry. My grandfather and my grandmother need me. They are growing old."

Mandie smiled and teasingly asked, "Not even Dimar?"

Sallie's mouth opened wide in surprise. "What impossible things you say, Amanda Shaw! What about you? Are you going to marry Joe Woodard when you grow up?"

Mandie sobered at that question and said thoughtfully, "I just don't know. I keep telling him that by the time we are grown we will have met lots of other people and we could both be interested in someone else. And, of course, he says he'll never change his mind. Besides, I might decide I'd rather stay single."

"Then you had better tell Joe not to get your father's house back for you because you promised him if he would, you would marry him," Sallie told her.

Mandie smoothed out the curtain hem she had stitched and said, "I'm not sure he'd ever be able to do that. And when he grows older, he might decide not to become a lawyer."

"That is correct. We can never see into the future," Sallie remarked.

"If I could see all the nice things in my future, it would be fun, but I wouldn't want to see all the bad things that might happen to me," Mandie said.

"If we could see into the future we would be able to change some things we did not like," Sallie said.

Mandie looked up from her sewing and said, "If we could see into the future, I would be able to solve all the mysteries I run into without getting into all the trouble I encounter." She paused. "But, no, that wouldn't be any fun at all. I'm glad God made us without a future memory, or whatever you call it."

"I am glad, too," Sallie agreed. She got up to add a log to the fire in the big open fireplace. "It is getting late. My grandfather should have returned by now."

"Maybe he and Jessan stayed to visit awhile with Uncle Wirt and Aunt Saphronia," Mandie suggested.

"They may not be able to find your uncle Wirt," Sallie said as she sat down and resumed her sewing.

Mandie looked at her with concern. "I hope he had come home from wherever he went by the time Uncle Ned and Jessan got to his house," she said. "Otherwise, how will they ever find him this time of the night?"

At that moment Morning Star came rushing in the front door. She began speaking in Cherokee to Sallie and gesturing with her hands. Sallie stood up to listen. Mandie couldn't understand the language, but she could sense immediately that something was wrong. She also got up from her seat at the table where the curtains lay.

"What is it?" Mandie asked, trying to interrupt the woman and Sallie.

Morning Star finally finished and Sallie said,

"Your uncle Wirt was not at his house and no one knows where he is—"

"Oh, no," Mandie interrupted.

"My grandfather and Jessan have asked others to help, and they will be searching for him until they find him," Sallie continued.

"What can we do to help?" Mandie asked as she thought of the old man who was her father's uncle.

"There is nothing we can do, Mandie. We cannot go out alone this time of the night," Sallie replied.

Morning Star began speaking Cherokee to Sallie again. Mandie listened intently but could not interpret a single word. Sallie answered a couple of times.

Finally Sallie turned to Mandie and asked, "Do you want to go to Tsa'ni's mother's house to wait with her until Jessan comes back? All the women are going to sit with her and I have convinced my grandmother that you and I are old enough now to join in the wait."

"Yes, I would, Sallie. I'd like to know when they find Uncle Wirt," Mandie said. "I want to be sure he is all right."

Sallie spoke to her grandmother, and Morning Star turned and went back out the front door. Snowball stirred on the hearth, curled up, and went back to sleep.

"We must get wraps. Remember, it is cold here in the mountains late at night," Sallie told Mandie.

The girls hurried upstairs to the bedroom. Sallie took a heavy shawl from a hook on the wall and Mandie pulled a cape out of her valise. They went back outside and quickly walked down the road to the house of Tsa'ni's mother. Bright moonlight showed wagons and carts parked all over the yard. They could smell strong coffee in the air.

"Looks like everybody is here," Mandie commented as they walked up to the front door. Some of the women were sitting on the stoop outside, and the huge room inside was filled with more women. Meli was filling cups with coffee from a pot over the fire in the fireplace.

Most of the people knew who Mandie was and they nodded as the girls entered the house. Sallie spoke to the women she passed but went straight to Meli. Morning Star was sitting near the fire.

"I will ask if we can help with the coffee," Sallie said to Mandie and then spoke in Cherokee to Meli.

Meli smiled at the girls and handed each of them a cup. Sallie turned back to Mandie and said, "She said we could get our own. Everyone else has some now."

Sallie filled Mandie's cup and then her own. "Remember, it is hot," she reminded Mandie as they began working their way through the crowd. "If we can get to the backdoor steps, we can sit there. I do not see anyone back there." Mandie carefully carried her cup, which she noticed Sallie had fortunately not filled completely full, and watched as she stepped through the crowd in order not to bump into anyone.

They made it safely to the back door and sat down on the steps. Mandie pulled up her long skirts and set the cup by her feet. "Whew!" she sighed loudly. "I'm glad I don't have to do that very often."

Sallie laughed and said, "Yes."

Mandie turned sideways to lean against the doorframe so she could look back into the room. "I was just thinking about Aunt Saphronia," she said. "I know she's not here and I was wondering if she's sitting home by herself worrying about Uncle Wirt."

"No, she will not be alone," Sallie said. "The

women of Bird-town will be sitting in wait with her.''

"I wish it wasn't so far so I could go to her house,'' Mandie remarked. "I feel helpless, and I'm really worried about Uncle Wirt.''

"My grandfather will find him,'' Sallie promised.

"I know Uncle Wirt must be awfully old, because he is my grandmother Shaw's brother,'' Mandie remarked. "He's too old to go off like this without letting someone know.''

"But do not forget. He is also Cherokee, and Cherokee men stay well and live long lives,'' Sallie said with a smile.

"Do you know if he has ever just disappeared before?'' Mandie asked as she sipped the hot coffee and wrapped her cold fingers around the cup. It was beginning to get chilly. She huddled up in the folds of the her cape.

"I do not know,'' Sallie replied as she warmed her fingers around her mug. She pulled the shawl she wore closer around her shoulders. "Maybe we should get closer to the fire,'' she suggested.

Mandie glanced back into the huge room. The crowd was thick and she couldn't see a vacant space anywhere. "I don't think there's enough room for us,'' she replied with a laugh. "But I have an idea. Why don't we go back to your house so I can check on Snowball? You know we left him asleep by the fire, and your fire may need some more wood. After we add some, we could come back here.''

Sallie stood up. "All right, we will go check on Snowball,'' she said. "But the fire is all right, I am sure. The huge logs in it will burn for hours.''

Mandie got to her feet as she untangled her cape. "What should we do with our cups?'' she asked.

"Here. Leave them on the doorstep until we return," Sallie said, stooping to set her cup beside Mandie's on the steps.

"Let's go out the back way," Mandie said.

"Yes, it will be easier," Sallie agreed, and she followed Mandie down the stairs into the dark backyard.

The girls walked around the house to the roadway and hurried back to Uncle Ned's house.

"He's still asleep," Mandie said, approaching the white cat curled up on the hearth. "And the fire does look fine."

At that moment Snowball opened his eyes, looked up at his mistress, stood up, and stretched.

Sallie laughed. "You mean he *was* asleep," she said.

"Oh, shucks!" Mandie said. "I'd better take him with us, I suppose. I'll get his leash—it's upstairs. I don't want him running loose this time of the night." She went over to the ladder and started to climb upstairs.

"I will hold him until you get it," Sallie said, stooping to pick up the white cat.

"Be right back," Mandie said, and she disappeared upstairs.

Mandie took the red leash and collar from a nail in the wall of the bedroom where she and Sallie slept, and then she hurried back downstairs.

Sallie handed her the cat, and Mandie told him, "Now, Mr. Snowball, I'm going to fix you up so you can't run away." She quickly fastened the collar around his neck. Snowball looked at her and meowed as she set him down and held on to the end of the leash.

The girls walked back outside to return to Jessan's house. Just before they reached the road,

Sallie touched Mandie's arm and whispered, "I hear someone coming."

Mandie stopped to listen. She couldn't hear a thing. "Where?" she asked quietly.

"Someone is walking in the woods across the road and they are coming this way," Sallie explained as she tried to see into the darkness.

Mandie listened intently again. This time she could hear footsteps. The girls stood waiting anxiously and watching for whoever might appear. In a few moments, a tall figure came out onto the roadway. Mandie recognized the man right away. Scooping up Snowball, she ran to him and Sallie followed.

"Uncle Wirt! Uncle Wirt!" she called.

The figure stopped and turned to look back. His face was visible now—it really was her uncle Wirt. Mandie raced to his side and reached to clasp his old, wrinkled hand.

"Oh, Uncle Wirt, I am so glad to see you!" Mandie said, almost in tears, she was so happy. "Where have you been?"

The old man looked down at her in surprise. "Jim Shaw's papoose!" he exclaimed as he caught her other hand in his. The sudden movement made Mandie lose her grasp on Snowball's leash.

Sallie quickly picked up the white cat as she asked the man, "Are you all right?"

"Yes, yes," Uncle Wirt replied as he looked at Sallie. "What papooses doing out late this night?"

"Oh, you don't know what's going on," Mandie said quickly. "All the men are out looking for you, Uncle Wirt. You were supposed to go to see your son, Jessan, and you never got there. Where have you been?"

"Look for me?" Uncle Wirt asked in surprise.

"Need look for Tsa'ni. He took my horse."

"Tsa'ni took your horse?" Sallie asked.

"Why did he do that?" Mandie asked.

"Tsa'ni take me, show me men dig in mountain. We watch," Uncle Wirt said. "He take my horse to go tell Jessan. Not come back." The old man looked tired.

"You really saw the men digging up the mountain?" Mandie asked excitedly. "Where are they, Uncle Wirt?"

Uncle Wirt smiled down at her and said, "Long way. Other side of East Ridge. Now must find men looking for me."

"Yes, we must find my grandfather and tell him you are here," Sallie agreed.

"How will we find them?" Mandie asked. "Does anybody know where they went to look for Uncle Wirt?"

"My grandmother will know," Sallie said. "We must go ask her so we can tell everyone your uncle is here."

"Must find Tsa'ni, too, with my horse," Uncle Wirt said, and they started down the road toward Jessan's house.

Mandie took Snowball from Sallie and carried him. She did some thinking about what had happened as they hurried along. Tsa'ni probably took the old man's horse without intending to return with it. Uncle Wirt was Tsa'ni's grandfather. How could the boy be so mean?

As they entered Jessan's yard, everyone came hurrying to see the old man. There were cries of thankfulness. Meli greeted him at the door and said something in Cherokee. Uncle Wirt replied, and all the Cherokee women became silent as they listened to the conversation.

Sallie translated for Mandie, "He is telling her that Tsa'ni took his horse and did not return, and that he must now go find the men who are searching for him, to let them know he is here," she explained. "He is also saying they should find Tsa'ni, who has his horse."

Then Morning Star spoke to Uncle Wirt in Cherokee. Mandie asked Sallie, "Does your grandmother know where the men have gone to look?"

"She is saying my grandfather told her they would search by the hospital, and then by the schoolhouse, and then up the mountain on that side," Sallie explained.

Meli said something to the old man, and Sallie continued, "She has told him to take her cart and pony to find the men."

Mandie had a sudden idea. "Do you think we could go with him if he's going in the cart?" she asked in a whisper.

Sallie looked at her and then said, "My grandmother would have to give us permission to go." Sallie spoke rapidly in Cherokee to Morning Star.

Sallie's grandmother frowned, but finally smiled and nodded her head in approval as she told Sallie something in Cherokee.

Sallie turned to Mandie and said, "My grandmother says we may go if we want to stay up all night, but that we cannot sleep all day tomorrow. That would upset her mealtimes."

"That's all right with me. What about you?" Mandie quietly asked.

"If you wish to go, then I must go also," Sallie answered with a smile. She turned to her grandmother and spoke to her again in Cherokee, with a word now and then to Uncle Wirt. Mandie waited for the translation.

"I get cart and pony," Uncle Wirt said to Mandie. "Then we go. You wait here." He quickly left the room.

Sallie turned back to Mandie and said, "I told my grandmother that you wished to go and that I would also go, and that we would not sleep all day tomorrow—just perhaps a wink or two between meals." Her black eyes twinkled with merriment.

"Thanks, Sallie," Mandie replied. She looked at Snowball in her arms and added, "I suppose I'll have to take him, too."

The old man soon came back to the doorway and had the cart waiting outside.

The girls climbed up on the bench beside Uncle Wirt and they were off on a jolting ride over the bumpy mountain trails. Mandie held tightly to her white cat because Snowball didn't like the ride at all.

Mandie tried to carry on a conversation, but even her voice shook when she tried to speak. In fact, she believed even her teeth rattled as Uncle Wirt rushed the pony on over the roughest roads Mandie could remember seeing anywhere.

When they came to the hospital, Uncle Wirt slowed the pony and circled around the building. There was no sign of anyone.

"Are we going by the schoolhouse next, Uncle Wirt?" Mandie managed to ask during the slowed pace.

"Yes, we go to schoolhouse," Uncle Wirt told her. "No men here. We go to schoolhouse. Maybe men there. No Tsa'ni here with my horse either."

"Maybe we'll find Tsa'ni with the men, Uncle Wirt," Mandie said.

"Maybe," the old man muttered as he urged the pony ahead.

When Uncle Wirt pulled the cart up into the schoolhouse yard, Mandie perked up as she noticed lamplight coming from the window of Riley O'Neal's room. *He must still be up, even at this late hour,* she thought.

"Missionary O'Neal has a light in his room," Sallie remarked as she, too, looked toward the schoolhouse.

Uncle Wirt halted the pony as he said, "We ask missionary if he see men, also Tsa'ni." He quickly dropped the reins and stepped down from the cart.

Mandie and Sallie followed. As far as Mandie remembered, there was no outside door in Riley O'Neal's room, so it was necessary to go through the schoolroom to get there.

She saw that she must be right, because Uncle Wirt entered the schoolhouse and strode across the big room. As he tapped on the missionary's door, the door swung open by itself. The three glanced inside, but no one was there.

"He is probably with the men searching," Sallie told Uncle Wirt.

"Yes," the old man agreed.

Snowball gave an unexpected lunge over Mandie's arm and managed to jump to the floor of Riley O'Neal's room. When Mandie tried to reach for him, he immediately jumped up on a shelf and scattered a stack of papers.

Mandie hurried to catch the falling papers, and Sallie helped.

"Snowball, you are in trouble now," Mandie

told the cat as he sat there on the shelf watching his mistress. She stooped and began placing the papers in a stack on the floor. Fancy handwriting on what seemed to be a letter caught her eye. At the end of the page were the words, "I love you." And underneath was signed "Mary Lou."

"Here are the others," Sallie said as she dropped more papers on top of the ones Mandie had stacked.

Mandie sighed as the letter was covered. She knew she had no right to read another person's mail, but she couldn't help having seen the signature. She picked up the stack and silently wondered who Mary Lou was. Mandie thought she must be a girl friend, since she had written that she loved him.

"We go," Uncle Wirt told the girls.

Snowball began to walk and knocked his leash off the shelf. Mandie grabbed the leash hanging from the shelf and replaced the papers he had knocked down. Then she managed to pull the cat down into her arms.

"You've been bad," Mandie told Snowball as she followed Uncle Wirt and Sallie outside.

She thought about Mary Lou as they traveled on. *She's probably some stuck-up Boston girl,* she decided, since he was from that city. But she was puzzled as to why the girl would be stuck up. But then, Mandie knew nothing about Mary Lou, and she should put this out of her mind at once.

Chapter 6 / Night Riders

Uncle Wirt decided to circle the mountain beyond the schoolhouse and then head toward his
house in Bird-town. The terrain was steep and
rough, but the old man urged the pony on through
the dark woods.

Mandie squeezed Snowball with one hand and
gripped the seat with her other hand. She noticed
Sallie was clinging tightly to the cart with both
hands. Mandie was beginning to wonder how they
would ever hear the other men over the noise of the
cart if they came near them.

Uncle Wirt suddenly drew up the reins and
brought the cart to a stop on a steep incline. He
pulled up the creaky brake and handed the reins to
Sallie.

"Did you hear someone, Uncle Wirt?" Mandie
said, blowing out her breath in relief and straightening her long skirts.

Uncle Wirt stood up in the cart and smiled at

Mandie. Then he coupled his hands before his mouth and gave a loud bird call. Mandie recognized the sound as the one Uncle Ned used when he was looking for her. The old man did this several times, and he listened for an answer after each call. The girls waited silently.

"Not here," Uncle Wirt finally said, retrieving the reins and sitting down. "Try again up mountain."

Mandie braced herself and Snowball as Uncle Wirt urged the pony on. She happened to glance to her left, into a clearing filled with moonlight. Someone wearing white flitted through the area. She was positive she had seen someone this time, but it would be impossible to make herself heard above the rattle and rush of the cart, so she didn't try to mention it to Sallie or Uncle Wirt.

"Someone in white clothes is definitely following us—or me—around," Mandie said quietly to herself. "Who could it be? It was too dark to tell whether it was a man or woman, but it could have been Tsa'ni."

Uncle Wirt stopped the cart several times on the way, and when they reached the top of the mountain, he pulled up the reins. From the clearing at the top, Mandie looked out over a large valley, brightly illuminated by the moon.

"We rest," he told the girls as he stepped down from the cart and tied the reins to a nearby sapling. He walked over to the edge of the clearing to gaze down the mountainside.

"Whew! We've sure been in a fizz!" Mandie exclaimed as she clutched Snowball and quickly jumped the short distance to the ground, with Sallie right behind her.

"My knees are wobbly!" Mandie said, laughing as she stomped her feet.

"I am wobbly all over," Sallie said. She stretched and bent and suddenly yawned.

"Uh-huh, these late hours are catching up with you," Mandie teased. She let Snowball walk around at the end of his leash.

Sallie laughed. "Since we stayed awake talking last night and riding tonight, I think I am beginning to be a little sleepy," she said as she walked about.

"Sallie, I saw someone in white back down in the clearing when we first stopped," Mandie told her.

Sallie stopped to look at her. "Are you sure this time?" she asked.

"Yes, I am positive. I know I saw someone run through an open space down there as we pulled off the path. The cart was so noisy and bumpy I didn't try to tell you then," Mandie said as Snowball kept walking circles around her. She had to keep turning to avoid having the leash wrap around her ankles. "And whoever it was rushed by so fast I couldn't tell whether it was a man or woman. You know what I think? I believe it's Tsa'ni trying to play tricks on us."

Sallie frowned and asked, "But why would Tsa'ni do that?"

"I don't know, but he does a lot of things that just don't make sense," Mandie replied. "Evidently he is hiding from me *and* from Uncle Wirt, now that he has Uncle Wirt's horse."

Suddenly Uncle Wirt, standing at the edge of the clearing, began sending his bird calls again. The girls became silent because they both knew they should be helping the old man listen for any answer he might get. There was only silence after the echo of his calls died away.

The old man sighed in disappointment, and returned to the cart. "We go now," he told the girls as he untied the reins and stepped up to the seat.

Mandie and Sallie followed him. They took their places, one on each side of Uncle Wirt. Mandie held tightly to Snowball with one arm and wrapped his leash around her wrist. "Where could everyone be?" Mandie asked Uncle Wirt as he tightened the reins.

"We find," he replied, smiling at her. "We go my house now."

"You are right," Sallie told him. "The men have had time to get all the way to your house."

"We see," he said as he shook the reins, and the pony began moving down the mountainside.

Mandie almost held her breath as Uncle Wirt guided the animal down the steep terrain. Sometimes she was afraid the cart was going to run into the pony's backside as it sped forward. Then, suddenly, the cart gave a lurch and tilted sideways. As they grabbed for something to hold on to, Mandie realized what had happened. The cart had lost a wheel here in the middle of nowhere—on a dangerous mountainside in the dark.

Uncle Wirt expertly brought the pony to a stop as he jumped down from the cart. The girls followed him. They found the wheel lying in the bushes nearby, and Uncle Wirt spoke rapidly in Cherokee. Mandie could hear anger in his voice.

"What is he saying?" Mandie whispered to Sallie.

Sallie shook her head and said in a low voice, "He is saying the spirits are angry tonight."

Uncle Wirt retrieved the wheel, examined it, and then looked at the axle. "Lost pin," he muttered as he began looking about in the darkness.

"A pin, Uncle Wirt?" Mandie asked. "We'll help if you'll tell me what kind of a thing we are looking for."

Uncle Wirt looked at her in the moonlight and said, "Sallie, show pin in other wheels." He continued searching the ground.

Sallie tried to show Mandie what a pin looked like in the other wheels, but it was so dark Mandie only got the idea that it was something straight that held the wheel on to the axle.

"I do not think we can find it in the darkness in all this underbrush," Sallie said. "But we can try."

"Sallie, if we don't find it we'll have to walk all the way down the mountain, won't we? And we must be a long ways from Uncle Wirt's house." She held on to Snowball and tried to look for the pin.

"Yes, it would be a long way to walk," Sallie agreed as she bent over and crept about in the darkness.

After a while, Uncle Wirt straightened up and looked at the girls. "Now we walk," he announced, unhitching the pony and holding the reins as he turned to begin the descent through the bushes as a shortcut. "Follow me. Stay close."

Mandie pulled her cape up tight around herself to keep from stumbling. She partly covered Snowball with it. Sallie lifted her shawl to cover her head, but it was still long enough to touch her skirt. The bushes were too thick to walk side by side. Sallie motioned for Mandie to get in the middle, right behind Uncle Wirt who was leading the pony. Sallie brought up the rear.

The journey was slow and tedious. Now and then Uncle Wirt would call a halt and send out his bird calls. The only response was silence. Mandie noticed that they seemed to be going down the mountain at an angle. "Why don't we just go straight down? It would save a lot of steps," she asked Sallie over her shoulder.

"It is too steep to go straight," Sallie explained. "The pony could slip or go too fast to hold him back."

"I suppose you're right," Mandie agreed. She glanced through a clearing down the mountainside and to her right. Through the moonlight she saw a road. Looking back at Sallie, she exclaimed, "Look! There's a road right down there." But as she turned to look at the road again, she suddenly lost her footing and began sliding down the steep grade. Mandie was unable to grasp anything on the way down and in an instant found herself lying in the road below.

She immediately noticed a wagon bearing down on her in a hurry. She screamed, "Stop," as she tried to untangle herself from her cape. She could hear Sallie and Uncle Wirt calling to her from above.

The vehicle came nearer, and Snowball managed to pull free and bounce out of the tangled cape into the road. The wagon came to a screeching halt. Someone reached down to uncover Mandie as she fought her way out of the folds of her cape. She looked straight into the blue eyes of Riley O'Neal, who was holding a lantern above her.

Getting to her feet she exclaimed, "Not you again!"

"And I would say, not again," the missionary said with a smile. "Are you all right?"

"Oh, yes, I'm all right," Mandie said, feeling embarrassed as she tried to straighten her clothes and hide her scratched hands at the same time.

"That's good but, you know, you seem to have a habit of falling in front of my wagon," he teased, reminding her of the first time he had met her.

Uncle Wirt, still leading the pony, and Sallie finally caught up with Mandie.

"Papoose hurt?" the old man questioned her.

"Mandie, are you all right?" Sallie asked at the same time.

Mandie smiled at them and said, "I'm all right." She waved her hand at Riley O'Neal and said, "I even got us a ride!"

"May I ask where you are going this time of the night?" the missionary inquired as he looked at the old man and the pony.

"We look for men who look for me," Uncle Wirt tried to explain. "Cart broke up mountain."

Mandie saw the puzzled look on the missionary's face and explained that all the men had been looking for Uncle Wirt. "Didn't you know about all this? We came by your room at the schoolhouse and there was a lamp burning, but you weren't there. We figured you were hunting for Uncle Wirt, too."

"No, I'm sorry, but I didn't know. You see, I had to go back to the depot for more supplies that came in on the train. That's why I'm out on the road so late," the young man explained. Then he frowned and asked, "You say there was a lamp lit in my room? I've been gone since way before dark, and I certainly didn't leave the lamp burning."

Sallie and Mandie looked at each other. Uncle Wirt, who had tied the pony to a nearby tree, said, "Maybe men look for me and light lamp so you can see when you get home. You not have fireplace for light from fire like Cherokees do. No fire in your fire-place."

Riley O'Neal smiled at him and said, "You're right. I didn't remember to start a fire in the fireplace before I left. It's going to be awfully cold when I get home." He laughed. "But what are we doing standing out here on the road in the middle of the night? Where are you headed? I'll give you a ride."

"We go to my house. See if men there," Uncle Wirt told him.

"Then let's get on our way. Climb in," the missionary told them as he led the way with the lantern.

Mandie started to walk toward the wagon when she suddenly remembered Snowball. "Oh, where is Snowball?" she cried, looking about the road. "Snowball, where are you? Snowball!" The others began searching too. The missionary swung his lantern here and there in the search.

They walked near the pony and Mandie stopped to ask, "Uncle Wirt, are you going to leave the pony out here tied to that tree?"

"Yes, pony be all right. Come back later," the old man explained.

Riley O'Neal turned to look at the old man and said, "Mr. Pindar, you go ahead and get in the wagon and rest a while. We only have one lantern, so there's no use all four of us looking together."

"You look, I rest. Then you rest, I look," the old man agreed, then he turned, walked back to the wagon, and climbed up on the seat.

"Snowball, where are you? Come here, Snowball!" Mandie called into the darkness of the hillside.

The three searched the road and the nearby area and Mandie kept calling Snowball. They worked their way back to the wagon to look in the bushes nearby, but he was nowhere to be found.

"Snowball, you'd better come here, right this minute," Mandie called loudly.

Suddenly she heard his meow. She quickly looked about. The meow grew louder. All at once Snowball jumped down from the back of the wagon and came running toward her. Everyone laughed.

"All this time you've been in the wagon!" Mandie exclaimed as she snatched him up and looked into his face.

"Evidently Snowball wanted to be sure he didn't get left," Riley O'Neal said with a laugh. "Now that we're all here, let's get going."

Mandie and Sallie climbed into the back of the wagon, and Mandie held tightly to her cat. Uncle Wirt sat on the seat with Riley O'Neal as they hurried down the road.

Mandie smelled the chimney smoke from the many fireplaces before they reached Bird-town. She could also hear the sound of many people talking after they finally rounded the bend and the village came into view.

Sallie leaned forward. "Your uncle Wirt was right. The men are here. There is my grandfather's horse," she said, pointing to an animal tethered by the road. Riley O'Neal pulled his wagon into the yard of Uncle Wirt's house.

"Oh, thank goodness!" Mandie said, letting out a loud sigh as the cart came to a stop. People came running to surround the wagon. Mandie and Sallie managed to slide down to the ground in spite of the crowd.

"We look. We look everywhere," Mandie could hear Uncle Ned telling her uncle Wirt.

"And we look and we look," Uncle Wirt said with a tired laugh as he alighted from the wagon.

Aunt Saphronia pushed her way through the crowd. She took Uncle Wirt's hand and said, "Come. Coffee." She looked at the girls and the missionary, then added, "You, too. Coffee. Cold out here."

Mandie, holding tightly to Snowball, along with Sallie, and Riley O'Neal followed the old man and woman into the house. Mandie could hear her uncle telling the others about Tsa'ni taking his horse and not coming back, and then about the accident with the cart. Everyone nodded sympathetically.

Aunt Saphronia took cups from a shelf and poured coffee from a kettle over the fire in the fireplace. She passed it to the girls and the missionary. The three of them hovered near the fire as Uncle Wirt and Aunt Saphronia sat down nearby and conversed in Cherokee.

The women who had been sitting in wait with Aunt Saphronia and the men who had been searching for Uncle Wirt bid them good-night and began leaving. Some of them had a long ride back to their homes in Deep Creek.

Mandie saw Uncle Ned speak to Uncle Wirt, and Sallie translated for Mandie and Riley O'Neal. She said, "My grandfather is telling your uncle Wirt that we need to go home and let the women know he is safe."

"But how are we going to get home? Your grandfather rode his horse, remember? And we had to leave your mother's cart in the mountains," Mandie reminded her.

Riley O'Neal spoke up as he sipped the hot coffee, "Oh, but I will take you home of course."

"But Uncle Ned doesn't live really close to where you do," Mandie said. She held the coffee cup with one hand and held Snowball's leash with the other. "You came this far out of your way. You'll never get home tonight."

Riley O'Neal looked straight at her with a teasing smile and said, "Neither will you. The night is gone—I just heard a rooster crow."

At that moment, Mandie heard the rooster and she said with a worried look, "Oh, I do hope we get home in time for breakfast." She looked at Sallie and added, "You know your grandmother always wants us home when it's time to eat."

Sallie said, "She will understand this time." She paused to listen to the conversation between her grandfather and Uncle Wirt. "My grandfather is telling your uncle Wirt they will get the cart and the pony from the mountain when it has become daylight, then they will go looking for Tsa'ni, who has your uncle Wirt's horse."

Uncle Ned stopped talking and looked toward the girls and the missionary. Riley O'Neal stepped forward to speak to him. "Whenever you are ready, I will take all of you home in my wagon. Would you like to leave your horse or ride with us?"

Uncle Ned nodded and said, "You take papooses. I take horse, ride by wagon."

The missionary agreed.

Mandie quickly put her cup on a nearby shelf and picked up Snowball. She was tired and ready to get back to Uncle Ned's house. Sallie and Riley O'Neal placed their cups beside Mandie's.

After quick good-nights, the girls climbed up on the seat of the wagon with Riley O'Neal, and Uncle Ned brought his horse alongside. Mandie wrapped the cape tightly around her in the cold night air and held tightly to Snowball, who was sitting in her lap.

Streaks of light were cracking the black sky, and birds could be heard singing all around them. Mandie, Sallie, and Mr. O'Neal were all sleepy, but they forced themselves to stay awake with conversation about nothing important. Mandie was thinking about how good her bed would feel, but kept reminding herself that Morning Star had told her and Sallie they would not be allowed to sleep the day away if they stayed up all night. She hoped Morning Star would change her mind about that.

"I am glad that everything turned out well," Sallie remarked from where she sat beside Riley O'Neal.

"Yes, I suppose it finally did," Mandie agreed. "Of course there are lots of loose ends to tie up. We still haven't found Tsa'ni, and now he has Uncle Wirt's horse. And we still haven't seen the strange men."

"Neither have I," Riley O'Neal said. "And I'm beginning to think maybe Tsa'ni made up this story about men digging. No one else seems to have seen them."

"Oh, you haven't heard," Mandie said quickly. "That's where my uncle Wirt was when Tsa'ni took his horse—watching the strange men with Tsa'ni. There really *are* men digging up the mountain. I think we need to find them and put a stop to it."

Riley O'Neal looked at her quickly and said, "That is no job for you or me. The Cherokee people will take care of these men, I am sure."

"Yes, my grandfather said they would," Sallie told him, and she glanced back to make sure Uncle Ned was still riding his horse behind the wagon.

"When we get home, you ask my grandfather about them."

"But I am one-fourth Cherokee. Why can't I help?" Mandie protested.

"But you do not live here with the Cherokee people," Sallie reminded her. "It is our mountain these men are digging up and it is for our men to stop them."

"Well, I'd like to at least get a glimpse of them," Mandie said.

"Maybe you will be able to do that," Sallie said.

"I'd just like to know what they are doing," Mandie said. "I can't imagine why they would be digging all over the mountain."

"Unless they are maybe digging to put a road through the mountain," Riley O'Neal suggested as they rode along.

"Put a road through the mountain?" Mandie asked. "Why, that would take forever. It's so steep and rocky."

"Yes, it would take years, perhaps," Sallie agreed.

"Or maybe they plan to run a railroad through the mountain," Mr. O'Neal said.

"But they cannot do that," Sallie said. "It is not their mountain."

"Maybe your grandfather knows more about it now that all the men searched the mountain for Amanda's uncle Wirt," the missionary said.

"We will ask my grandfather," Sallie replied.

Mandie wondered about the strange men. Everyone was talking about them, but no one seemed to have any plans to really find out what they were doing. If she could get half a chance, she would locate these men and see for herself what they were doing. She would find out what it was all about.

Chapter 7 / Who Lit the Fire?

On the way to Uncle Ned's, Riley O'Neal drove his wagon by Jessan's house. As he passed it, he pulled up on the reins and stopped.

"Looks like almost everybody has gone home," Mandie remarked as Uncle Ned drew his horse up beside the wagon.

"Wait," the old Indian told Riley. Uncle Ned dismounted and hurried toward the open door.

Mandie, Sallie, and Riley watched as Uncle Ned looked inside the doorway and quickly came back to the wagon.

"Jessan take shortcut. Home now," the old man explained. "Morning Star go home. We go too." He mounted his horse and led the way down the road to his home.

Having arrived, he again dismounted and spoke to Riley O'Neal. "We thank you, bring papooses home," he said, shaking hands with the missionary, who stayed on the wagon seat. "Come. Eat," Uncle Ned added.

Riley shook his head and replied, "Some other time. I'll go on home now and get this wagon unloaded. But thank you anyway."

Sallie jumped down from the wagon. Mandie did the same, and Snowball remained asleep in her arms in spite of the jolt.

"Uncle Ned, we all wanted to ask you about the strange men," Mandie began.

"We talk later, not now. Go wash, eat," he told the girls.

Riley O'Neal bid them goodbye and drove out into the road. Mandie sighed and followed Sallie into the house as Uncle Ned took his horse to the backyard.

Evidently, Mandie thought, *Uncle Ned is not going to discuss the strange men.*

Morning Star was busy stirring food in the kettle over the fire in the fireplace. She started speaking to Sallie in Cherokee as soon as Mandie and Sallie entered the room. Mandie stopped to listen as Sallie answered in her language but, as usual, she couldn't understand a thing they were saying. She dropped the sleeping cat onto the hearth. He meowed, stretched slowly to his feet, walked around in a circle, and then curled up to sleep again.

"My grandmother and I were talking about your uncle Wirt and where we had been," Sallie explained as the two girls went to the shelf to wash in the basin there.

Morning Star spoke loudly to the girls as Uncle Ned came in the back door. "Wash. Eat. Sleep," she said, smiling.

Mandie gave a sigh of relief knowing they were going to be allowed to sleep.

"Little sleep," the old woman added as she looked at the girls.

"Yes, my grandmother," Sallie said as she dried her face and hands on a towel hanging on a nail by the basin.

Mandie did likewise and asked Sallie, "How much is a little sleep?"

Sallie smiled and explained, "I think we may be able to sleep until it is time to eat again at noon. Then we must help my grandmother with the food because she has also stayed up all night."

"Of course," Mandie agreed, walking toward the table with Sallie. "Just between you and me, I'd much rather go to bed than eat right now, but since your grandmother has already prepared breakfast, I wouldn't dare tell her that."

"She has always insisted that we eat before we sleep," Sallie said as the girls took their seats at the table across from Uncle Ned.

Morning Star brought them bowls of steaming food from the kettle at the fireplace and then sat down beside her husband.

Mandie was too sleepy to even ask what she was going to eat, but when she took a spoonful of the soupy mixture, she decided it was corn soup. It was delicious. She ate it all, and some bean bread.

No one spoke during the meal, and when they were all finished, Uncle Ned stood up and said, "Sleep now. Then we go get cart and pony." He left the room without another word.

The girls cleared the table quickly, while Morning Star put scraps on a plate and set it before Snowball. He immediately stood up, stretched, and sniffed the food. Then he hastily devoured it and licked the plate clean.

When they were finished, the girls went upstairs to sleep. They were both too tired to talk or even undress, so they lay down with their clothes on and fell asleep. Snowball joined them, lying down next to Mandie on the bed.

The next thing the girls knew, Morning Star was calling up the ladder to the room where they slept. "Eat. Eat now," she was saying.

Mandie sat up quickly and Sallie rolled out of bed and onto her feet.

"Oh, we didn't help with the food," Mandie said, sliding off the bed and straightening her clothes. "Seems like we just went to sleep." She yawned and pushed back stray tendrils of her blond hair.

"We will clear the table and wash the dishes after we eat," Sallie told her, then they both turned to hurry down the ladder.

When she reached the bottom rung and looked into the kitchen, Mandie saw Snowball following Morning Star around the room, rubbing against her long skirts. "Sallie, look at that cat," Mandie said with a laugh. "He must have smelled food before we even woke up."

"Yes," Sallie agreed with a smile. She hurried to the fireplace where her grandmother was filling bowls. Mandie followed.

Morning Star turned and said sternly, "Sit." And she continued filling the bowl she held.

Mandie looked at Sallie, who nodded toward the table. The girls went to sit down,

"My grandmother does not like for other people to do her work," Sallie explained. "But she will not mind if we clear the table."

"That's good, because I feel that I should be doing something," Mandie said as Uncle Ned came in and joined them at the table. "Good morning, Uncle Ned," she greeted him.

"Noon now," the old man said with a smile.

Mandie had been sleepy when they had found the search party at Uncle Wirt's house, and she didn't remember seeing Dimar in the crowd. Now she asked Uncle Ned, "Did Dimar go with you men to look for Uncle Wirt?"

"Yes, Dimar good boy," Uncle Ned replied, and Morning Star set a bowl in front of him. "Jerusha, mother of Dimar, go home. Dimar take mother home."

"So that's why Dimar was not at Uncle Wirt's house with all the men," Mandie said.

She looked at the bowl Morning Star had given her and could tell immediately by the delicious aroma that it held chicken stew. "M-m-m-m! I love it!" she said, breathing in the steam from the bowl. She waited until Morning Star had served Sallie and herself, then sat down as Uncle Ned returned thanks. After that, Mandie hungrily ate the stew.

Just as they finished the stew, Mandie heard the rattle of a wagon and the clop of horse hooves outside. A minute later, Jessan appeared in the doorway.

"We go now," Uncle Ned told the girls as he rose from the table.

"But we need to help Morning Star clear the table," Mandie protested as she pointed at the dishes on the table.

Morning Star evidently understood Mandie's gesture, for she shook her head and said loudly, "Go. Go."

Mandie frowned, grabbed Snowball's leash from a nail where she had hung it, and fastened it to his collar. Carrying her cat, she reluctantly followed Uncle Ned and Sallie out into the yard, where Jessan had gone to wait beside his wagon. Sallie looked at Mandie and said, "My grandmother understands we must go when my grandfather says go. Do not worry."

The girls climbed into the back of the wagon as the men took seats on the bench up front. Jessan shook the reins and the horse pulled the wagon out into the road. Mandie tied Snowball's leash to a hook on the side of the wagon bed.

Uncle Ned looked back and told the girls, "Help watch. We find cart and pony. Wirt tired last night and not able to remember exact place."

"I know where, my grandfather," Sallie assured him. "The missionary was passing in his wagon on the Tellico Road when he found us. The pony is tied up there, and the cart is above that with a lost wheel."

Uncle Ned nodded and spoke to Jessan. The rattle of the wagon and the clopping of the horse drowned out their conversation.

Mandie suddenly felt herself nodding away. She shook her head and sat up straighter. How could she doze during such a rough ride! She glanced at Sallie and saw that she had slid down onto a blanket and had her eyes closed. Snowball was curled up asleep on the corner of the blanket.

Thank goodness Jessan was not dozing as he drove the wagon! And Uncle Ned was alertly watching the scenery as they rode on. Then all at once Uncle Ned called out. "Slow. There!" he said to Jessan as he pointed ahead.

Mandie looked ahead as Jessan slowed the wagon. Yes, there was the pony, still tethered to the tree where they had left him. Uncle Ned jumped down when Jessan stopped the wagon. He hurried to the pony and began rubbing its head as he spoke to it.

Sallie awoke and sat up. She looked at Mandie and explained, "The poor pony has been out all night away from home. My grandfather is comforting the animal."

Mandie understood what Sallie said. Uncle Ned was such a good, kind person. Even the comfort of his animals was important to him.

The old Indian stepped up to the side of the wagon and asked Sallie, "Which way cart?"

Sallie pointed up the mountainside. "There, my grandfather, up that way. I will show you," she said as she jumped down from the wagon. Looking back at Mandie, she added, "Come." Mandie picked up Snowball and caught up with Sallie.

Jessan tied the reins of his horse to a bush nearby and followed the others up the mountainside. The girls scrambled through the undergrowth and before long had located the cart.

Uncle Ned bent to look at the axle and then looked around the area. "Find wheel," he said.

Jessan spotted the wheel behind some thick bushes. He rolled it up to the cart while Uncle Ned examined the wheel and said, "Tools. Fix."

The younger man understood and rushed off to his wagon to bring the tools up to the cart.

"Can you fix it, Uncle Ned?" Mandie asked as the old Indian looked closely at the axle on the cart.

"Think can, Papoose," Uncle Ned said.

"I'm glad it can be repaired," Mandie replied.

Snowball walked around her feet as she held the end of his red leash.

"Yes, and my grandmother will be glad to have her cart fixed, too," Sallie said.

Jessan got back with the tools, and he helped Uncle Ned put the wheel on the cart. When they had finished, Uncle Ned declared it was "fit to roll." He and Jesse began pulling the cart down the mountainside through the bushes toward the waiting pony. The girls followed. Mandie carried Snowball, just in case he decided to run away.

Once the men had the pony hitched to the cart, Uncle Ned told the girls, "Now we go see place arrow shot at papooses with Dimar." He motioned for Mandie and Sallie to get into his cart.

As they climbed up into the cart Mandie told Sallie, "I hope you know how to find the place. I sure don't."

"I am not sure," Sallie replied. She turned to her grandfather and said, "We must get Dimar to show you the place, my grandfather. I am not familiar with the paths he took us on."

"We get Dimar," Uncle Ned replied.

But Jessan reminded him, "We got business to go to. Late now."

Uncle Ned thought for a moment and then said, "We must do this now. We get Dimar. Not take long time. You go in wagon. I go in cart. We go to house of Dimar. He show us place. Then I go with you. Dimar take cart and papooses home."

Mandie was glad that Uncle Ned would leave them with Dimar, because she knew he liked to explore any ideas she came up with.

Uncle Ned flicked the reins against the pony and

led the way. With the girls in his cart, Jessan followed with the wagon.

Mandie was surprised to find out they were only a short distance from Dimar's house. When they arrived, Dimar was in the yard. Uncle Ned stopped, got off the cart, and explained what they wanted. The young man was glad to oblige. He smiled at the girls as he nodded agreement to Uncle Ned.

"Yes, I will show you the place," Dimar told Uncle Ned. "I have not been back, but I will take you there."

"Then tell your mother," Uncle Ned said.

"My mother is away visiting this afternoon. I will go with you now," Dimar said.

Uncle Ned climbed back up on the seat of the cart. Dimar sat beside him, but he kept looking back at the girls as he directed the old Indian to the place where someone had shot arrows at them. Jessan continued to follow in his wagon.

Finally Dimar said, "This is near the place. Now we must walk to get there." He jumped down when Uncle Ned stopped the cart, and Dimar caught the reins that the old man tossed to him. He secured them on a small tree by the roadway while Jessan tied up his horse, still hitched to the wagon, beside the cart.

Dimar led them through dense woods up and down hills and valleys. When he finally came to a stop, Mandie looked around and recognized the place where they had been. The three of them explained to the men what they had been doing and what had happened.

Uncle Ned and Jessan began a careful search of the area. They looked at each tree trunk and then bent over to inspect every inch of the ground.

Mandie was following and carefully watching Uncle Ned when he suddenly found an arrow in the underbrush. He quickly picked it up to inspect it. After he had run his fingers over it, and turned it over and over, he shook his head.

"Not Cherokee arrow," he declared as he handed it to Jessan.

Jessan examined it thoroughly, gave it back to Uncle Ned, and agreed, "No, not Cherokee arrow."

"Well, if it's not a Cherokee arrow, what kind of an arrow is it, Uncle Ned?" Mandie asked as the two men stood thoughtfully looking at the arrow.

Uncle Ned blinked his black eyes, as though his mind had been far away, and he replied, "Not know, Papoose. Strange arrow."

"My grandfather, there are no other Indians on this mountain except the Cherokee," Sallie reminded the old man.

"My granddaughter, one who made this arrow may not live on this mountain," the old man explained.

Mandie remembered something and asked, "There were some Catawba Indians around here one time. They were dangerous men—outlaws, or something—remember?"

"Yes, Papoose," Uncle Ned said. "We keep arrow. We find who shot. Now we go."

Dimar led them back down to where they left the wagon and cart.

"I go with Jessan," Uncle Ned told the girls. "You go with Dimar. We go business. You go home."

Mandie suddenly had an idea as she and Sallie climbed into the cart with Dimar. "Uncle Ned, would it be all right if we go to see Riley O'Neal for a few minutes. We might be able to help him get something ready for the opening of school," she told him.

Uncle Ned hesitated a moment as he and Jessan sat in the wagon. "Few minutes only. Go home soon," he told Mandie. Looking at Sallie, he added, "My granddaughter, do not keep your grandmother wait for supper."

"We will go home for supper, my grandfather," Sallie promised.

The men went on their way and Dimar headed the cart toward the schoolhouse.

"Was there a special reason to visit the missionary?" Dimar asked Mandie.

"Well, you might say that," Mandie replied with a smile as she held Snowball in her lap. "You see, while y'all were out looking for Uncle Wirt last night, Sallie and I found Uncle Wirt, and we had to go looking for y'all to let you know. We went by the schoolhouse and there was a lamp burning in Riley O'Neal's room, but he was not home."

They passed over a bump and a sudden jolt jarred everyone. Mandie breathed a sigh of relief that the cart didn't lose a wheel again.

"Was he with some of the men? I did not see him," Dimar said as he expertly guided the cart down the road.

"No, he was gone to the Bryson City depot to get some more supplies that came in on the train, and he didn't even know about Uncle Wirt being missing until he met up with us early in the morning on Tellico Road."

Dimar looked at her and asked, "What were you doing on Tellico Road at night?"

Sallie spoke up with a sly smile, "That is where Mandie slid down the mountainside into the road in front of the missionary's wagon.''

Mandie blushed with embarrassment and she quickly explained that the cart had lost a wheel and the missionary gave them a ride, and it was then that they told Dimar about the lamp lit in Riley O'Neal's room. She added that the missionary had not lit the lamp and didn't know about it.

Dimar looked at Mandie and smiled as he asked, ''Who did light the lamp?''

''No one knows. That's why I want to go to see him—to ask him if he found out who lit the lamp,'' Mandie explained. ''It could have been those strange men who are digging up the mountain, you know.''

''That is a possibility,'' Dimar agreed. ''We will go ask the missionary about it.''

When Dimar pulled the cart up into the yard of the schoolhouse, Mandie was relieved to see the missionary's wagon parked nearby. He was probably home.

They found Riley O'Neal sitting at a table in the schoolroom and doing some paperwork. When they came through the doorway he stood up to greet them.

''Well, well, I hope you all had a nice nap after our late night,'' he said with a laugh, pushing back the red curls from his forehead,

''Oh, we did,'' Mandie said.

''I hope you slept some, too,'' said Dimar.

''Yes, and I do hope you had something to eat,'' Sallie added.

''I ate and I slept and then I ate again,'' the missionary said, still smiling. ''Sit down, have some seats over here.'' He motioned toward two benches at the end of the room.

Mandie tied the end of Snowball's leash to the leg of a table nearby, and they all sat down.

Mandie could wait no longer. She had to ask the question. "Did you find out who lit your lamp last night while you were gone?"

Riley looked at her and frowned as he said, "That's really a puzzle. You see, when I got home the lamp was not lit. I felt the wick and it was cold, so it must have been a while since the light was extinguished. However, the logs in my fireplace were burning and my room was nice and warm after that cold night air."

The three looked at him, puzzled.

"The lamp was not burning, but there was a fire in the fireplace. That's certainly strange," Mandie said.

"And you do not know who did this?" Dimar asked.

"Did you not see anyone around the schoolhouse when you returned?" Sallie asked.

"It's all a mystery to me," Mr. O'Neal said. "I didn't see anyone around then, and no one has been here today."

"Do y'all think it could have been the strange men who are digging up the mountain?" Mandie asked as she glanced at her friends.

"I do not believe they would be brave enough to come into the schoolhouse," Dimar said.

"Then, too, why would they do such a thing?" Riley asked.

"Maybe they were cold and needed a fire," Sallie suggested.

"Whoever did it must have been somewhere around here when Sallie and I came with Uncle Wirt, because the lamp was burning and the fireplace was cold then, but you said the lamp was not burning when you got home and you had a fire in the fireplace," Mandie said.

"Perhaps it was someone from the search party stopping by to warm up," Riley said. "It was terribly cold last night in these mountains."

"I was with the search party until we got to Wirt Pindar's house," Dimar said. "We passed here, but your wagon was gone so we did not stop. I do not remember whether there was a light in your window or not. I did not notice. But nobody entered."

"We may never know who was here," Riley said with a shrug.

Sallie rose as she reminded the others, "We have to go home. I promised my grandfather we would be there in time for supper."

The others stood up, and Mandie untied Snowball's leash, then picked him up.

"Is there anything we can help you with for the school before we go?" Mandie asked.

"Nothing right now," Riley replied with a big smile. "But all of you come back again anytime. We can discuss this mystery again." He laughed.

"Oh, don't worry," Mandie said. "We'll solve this mystery. We always do when we find one. We'll let you know who it was."

"Please do that," Riley said as he accompanied them to the front porch.

The three waved goodbye and rode off in the cart.

Mandie was really puzzled. There were actually two different incidents to consider: the lighting of the lamp *and* the fire in the fireplace. Maybe there were two different people involved. She couldn't imagine why anyone would light a lamp and then blow it out, but still leave a fire burning. All the men were out searching for Uncle Wirt, and all the women were sitting together, waiting for them to return.

Dimar looked at Mandie as she was deep in thought and said, "You will puzzle this out until you find an answer, will you not?"

"I just can't stand for things to be left at loose ends," Mandie said, grinning up at him as they rode along .

"And she never leaves the loose ends," Sallie added with a smile as she bent forward to look at Mandie on the other side of Dimar on the seat.

"Well, if I'm lucky, I don't leave any loose ends," Mandie said. "I'll find out who was at Mr. O'Neal's. You wait and see."

She sounded more confident than she felt. She had been forbidden to approach the strange men, but they were the ones she'd like to question. Somehow, some way, she'd figure it all out.

Chapter 8 / Snowball to the Rescue!

As the young people rode along in the cart en route to Uncle Ned's house, Dimar once again brought up the subject of Mandie's journey to Europe. He had been talking to other Cherokee people and now had a plan.

"Would it be agreeable to you if we set up a meeting on the schoolhouse grounds for you to tell us about Europe?" Dimar asked as he pulled on the reins to slow down the prancing pony, who was obviously glad to have been released from the tree.

"The schoolhouse grounds?" Mandie asked thoughtfully. Then she quickly added, "At night. We could have a big fire and we could have some food and—"

Dimar interrupted, "You make it sound like a festival."

"We will make it a festival," Sallie spoke up.

Dimar looked at both the girls and said, "Well, if you girls want to make it a festival, then we will call it a festival, and I will ask all the women to bring food. But you must decide where you want the fire built."

"Not too close to the schoolhouse, of course," Mandie said as she held on to Snowball in her lap. "And it would have to be in an open place so the trees and things wouldn't catch on fire. You pick the place. You know more about this than I do."

"All right," Dimar agreed. "I will pick the place tomorrow and will begin to send word around to prepare for this festival."

"Do you think people will really come—" Mandie began asking, but she was interrupted by a sudden exclamation from Sallie.

"Look! Look! There goes Tsa'ni!" she cried. She was pointing toward the mountain ridge to their right.

Dimar quickly stopped the cart, and Mandie stood up to look.

"It is Tsa'ni! Let's go follow him," Mandie cried as she jumped down from the cart, carrying Snowball in her arms.

"Mandie, we are supposed to be going home now," Sallie called to her.

Mandie didn't even look back. She left the roadway and began picking her way through the low bushes on the hillside.

Dimar looked at Sallie and sighed. "I suppose we had better follow her," he said. He jumped down and tied the reins to a bush as Sallie joined him.

The two quickly caught up with Mandie, and together they hurried in the direction Tsa'ni had gone. He had disappeared into the woods by then. Dimar walked ahead, beating bushes out of the way for the girls. Now and then they got a glimpse of Tsa'ni when he walked through a clearing. He seemed to be headed for the top of the ridge.

Soon Dimar had picked up his trail and was able to track him. Mandie watched as she walked behind. Dimar didn't miss a single clue, footprints here and there, broken twigs on bushes, trodden underbrush.

"How do you know this is Tsa'ni's trail? It could have been someone else going along here before, couldn't it?" Mandie asked between breaths as they started on an uphill pathway.

"I will explain to you later when we have more time, but you have to judge the newness of the broken twigs, whether time has allowed dust to settle over the footprints, and lots of other things," Dimar replied as they continued on.

Mandie thought about that, and she was also wondering where Tsa'ni was going. When the trail curved sharply to the right, she nearly fainted when Tsa'ni suddenly jumped out of the bushes in front of her. Dimar had already passed him.

"Tsa'ni!" was all Mandie could manage to say for a moment.

Sallie, who was walking behind her, nearly bumped into her when Mandie was stopped by Tsa'ni.

"So you finally found me!" he exclaimed as he stood there blocking the pathway.

"Tsa'ni, it is time you went home," Sallie admonished him.

Dimar had turned back and silently watched and listened.

"Where have you been, Tsa'ni?" Mandie asked as she tightened her grip on Snowball, who was now trying to get down. "You sent a message that you wanted to see me, and then you go and disappear. What is it you want with me?"

Tsa'ni tightened his lips and said through clenched teeth, "I wanted to show you what two of your white people are doing to our mountain. They are digging it up, piece by piece."

"Just because they are white doesn't mean that they are my people," Mandie replied. "As you well know, I am part Cherokee."

Dimar spoke then. "Who are these men, Tsa'ni? Have you seen them?"

Tsa'ni glared at Dimar for a moment, then finally answered, "Yes, I have seen them. I have been watching them for days and days, like every Cherokee ought to be doing. Here they are digging up our mountain, and nobody is trying to stop them."

"Uncle Ned said they plan to take action as soon as they find out what the men are up to," Mandie said.

"Where are these men now?" Sallie asked.

"Over that ridge there. I am on my way to see what they are doing now," Tsa'ni said.

"Could we go with you?" Mandie asked anxiously.

"I will not stop you from going to see them, but I warn you: Do not get too close," Tsa'ni said, fingering a rope coiled around his shoulders. "I plan to trap them with this rope and I do not wish to lose time trapping you also."

My grandfather has warned us to stay away from these men," Sallie told him. "He said they could be dangerous."

"Of course they are dangerous," Tsa'ni said. "They are white men trespassing on Cherokee land." Without another word, he turned and continued on his way up the ridge.

The three young people followed the Indian boy. When Tsa'ni came to an opening in the woods he suddenly stopped and waved for the others to stay behind him. Everyone was silent.

Mandie listened as they stood there. She could hear a clicking sound and a thump at regular intervals. She strained to see ahead. All the way across the clearing, two men were digging in great haste.

So those were the two strange men everyone was talking about. She couldn't see what they looked like because they both wore wide-brimmed hats and had their heads bent toward the ground, but she could tell one was an extraordinarily large man and the other one seemed to be much smaller.

"Stay here!" Tsa'ni said sternly. He crept through the bushes to the right, and Mandie knew at once that he was going to circle the woods and get on the other side of the clearing.

The three young people continued watching the men. Then suddenly the two strangers stopped digging, picked up their tools, and started walking to their left.

"They are leaving!" Mandie whispered to her friends.

"No, they are just changing places," Dimar whispered, and the men stopped a few feet from where they had been and started digging again.

"Yes," Sallie agreed.

"That makes no sense," Mandie said softly.

Suddenly Mandie spied Tsa'ni in the woods opposite her and her friends.

He had circled around the men, just as she had thought he would do. Then she watched as Tsa'ni stepped out into the clearing next to the men. At first the strangers didn't see him, but then he spoke.

"What are you doing to my mountain?" Tsa'ni demanded in a loud voice.

"Your mountain?" the large man questioned.

"Yes, my mountain. I am Cherokee, and this is Cherokee land," Tsa'ni told him. Mandie could see his fingers on the coiled rope. She was sure Tsa'ni would be no match for the two men. Why, the stupid boy might even be killed if he attacked the men with his rope. Snowball strained to get down from her arms and Mandie had a sudden idea.

"Snowball, go to those men," Mandie said, quickly setting Snowball down and removing his leash. She gave him a push from behind, but the cat needed no help. He was anxious to run. He went straight toward the strangers as Mandie and her friends watched.

"Go away, boy," the smaller man said to Tsa'ni. "Stop interfering in things that don't concern you."

"I will not go away. This does concern me," Tsa'ni said angrily, stepping toward the smaller man.

The larger man stopped digging and looked at Tsa'ni. "We happen to be government men. We are surveying for a map. We're drawing a map of this mountain. Now you get out of here," he said, motioning for Tsa'ni to get away from where they were digging.

As Tsa'ni stepped forward with the rope in his hands, Snowball ran across his path, causing him to stumble and lose his grip on the rope.

"You cat! Get!" Tsa'ni yelled at Snowball and tried to kick him.

Mandie was out of the bushes quick as a flash.

Tsa'ni had better not kick *her* cat. Besides, the man said they were government men. She wasn't afraid of them now. She raced across the clearing in pursuit of Snowball.

"Stop!" Mandie yelled at Tsa'ni as he tried to catch the cat. "Snowball, come here! Snowball!"

Snowball spun around, saw his mistress, and actually ran back to her. He usually ran away when she called to him. Mandie snatched him up and turned to look at the two men who had stopped digging to watch her. Tsa'ni stood at the edge of the clearing making angry signs with his hands. Dimar and Sallie followed Mandie as she walked toward the strangers.

"I heard you say y'all are government men," Mandie said as she stepped closer to the men.

"That's right. Now you just go back wherever you came from, miss, and take that Injun boy there with you," the big man said, pointing toward Tsa'ni.

"There's two more Injuns here," the smaller man said, looking toward Sallie and Dimar, who had stepped out of hiding by then.

Dimar came to stand in front of the big man. "What are you men doing?"

"I'm sure you heard me tell that other Injun boy that we are from the government, and we are surveying to make a map of this here mountain," the big man said. "Now that you know, go on back to your own business." He picked up his hoe and began digging again.

All the time they had been talking, Mandie was wondering how a person would go about making a map of a mountain. Was it necessary to do all the digging that these men had been doing? She didn't think so, unless they were putting up stakes, but she didn't see any stakes. Suddenly she realized they were lying, and she became afraid of them. She was sure they were dangerous, because she was sure they had lied.

"Come on, let's go," Mandie told Dimar and Sallie. Then looking across at Tsa'ni she called, "Let's go home, Tsa'ni."

Tsa'ni just stood looking at her, anger in his face.

"Come on, Tsa'ni. We want to talk to you," Dimar called to him.

"Please come walk with us, Tsa'ni. We have the cart at the bottom of the ridge," Sallie added.

Tsa'ni's face broke into a slight smile when he heard Sallie, and he began walking toward them. Mandie knew that Tsa'ni, for all his meanness, had a soft spot for Sallie, and now she was glad Sallie was able to persuade him away from the dangerous men.

Tsa'ni didn't speak when he caught up with the three, but continued to walk with them down the mountainside. No one spoke until they got to the cart.

Mandie leaned against the side of the cart and looked at her friends as she asked, "Y'all didn't really believe those men were government men, did you?" She turned to Tsa'ni to make sure he understood she was asking him too.

"I am not stupid," Tsa'ni said curtly.

"Then who are they?" Dimar asked.

"I believe they are crooks," Sallie said.

"I couldn't figure out what they were doing, digging a little in one place, and then moving on to another place so close by," Mandie said.

"I told you I have been watching them," Tsa'ni said. "That is all they do. They dig a little, move, dig a little more, move, and dig again." He looked at Snowball on Mandie's shoulder. "One day I am going to kill that white cat."

"If you ever want to make trouble, Tsa'ni, you just do that," Mandie said. "I can guarantee you that you will be sorry." She hugged Snowball close.

"Do you not realize that cat may have saved your life?" Dimar asked. "You were about to rope those men all by yourself and Snowball stopped you."

"I could take care of both of those men. They are fat and flabby," Tsa'ni bragged as he straightened his shoulders and drew himself up tall. "I will go back when they are not expecting it. I will stop them from digging up the mountain."

"If you try that, then you are really dumb, Tsa'ni," Mandie said.

Tsa'ni glared at her as he paced in front of them.

"We must go home now," Sallie reminded the others. "Tsa'ni, will you ride with us?"

Tsa'ni glanced at Sallie and said, "I can walk and get there faster than this old cart will go."

"But if you ride with us we will be able to talk," Sallie insisted.

Dimar spoke up, "Yes, do come with us, so we can discuss some things."

"Are you going home with Sallie, too?" Tsa'ni asked.

"Yes, I promised her grandfather I would take the girls home. My mother is visiting your mother, so I will be able to ride home in the cart with her," Dimar explained as he jumped into the cart. "Are you coming?"

Without another word, Tsa'ni climbed up onto the seat of the cart. Sallie and Mandie exchanged a secret smile and crawled into the back of the cart. Mandie held tightly to Snowball.

As Dimar hurried the pony down the rough road, Mandie suddenly remembered that Tsa'ni had taken Uncle Wirt's horse. Moving close to the back of the seat, she asked above the noise of the cart, "Tsa'ni, where is your grandfather's horse? He said you took it and never came back when y'all were watching those men dig. And he had to walk all the way down the mountain to your father's house."

Tsa'ni twisted around to look at her as he asked, "Does he not have his horse? I do not have it."

"He said you took it and never brought it back to him," Mandie argued. "What did you do with his horse, Tsa'ni?"

"I left the horse tied to a tree near where we were watching the men. I went back for it, but it was gone. So he took it," Tsa'ni said without looking at Mandie this time.

"No, he did not take it. He walked all the way home, and the men were all out searching for Uncle Wirt because no one knew where he was," Mandie said.

"Then someone else took the horse. I left it there," Tsa'ni insisted. "Probably the men who were digging up the mountain took the horse. I left it near them."

"Why did you leave the horse there instead of taking it back to Uncle Wirt?" Mandie asked. "Uncle Wirt said you were supposed to go tell your father where he was, and you never came back."

"I tell you, I left the horse up there," Tsa'ni said angrily. "Tomorrow I will go look for the animal."

Dimar asked, "Would you mind if I go with you tomorrow? Maybe we could get another look at those men and see if they are doing anything different."

Tsa'ni looked at Dimar and finally answered, "I do not care if you all go with me tomorrow. I plan to look alone for those men tomorrow."

"Do they not stay in any one particular area?" Dimar asked.

"No, they roam all over the mountain and they dig all day everywhere," Tsa'ni explained. "But they will not be digging anymore when I find out how to stop them."

"May I go with you, too?" Mandie asked.

Tsa'ni looked back at her and said, "It does not matter to me if you want to go up the mountain, but you had better keep that cat under control if you are with me or not. Remember that."

"I will help you take care of Snowball, Mandie," Sallie offered.

"Thanks, Sallie," Mandie said, smiling at her friend. "Do you think your grandmother and grandfather will allow us to go back up the mountain tomorrow?"

My grandfather may not be home tomorrow," Sallie said. "He and Jessan were planning to haul the crops to Asheville today, and they usually spend the night in Asheville—and sometimes even two nights there."

"Then we'll ask your grandmother," Mandie said.

"I do hope we get home by the time my grandmother has the supper cooked," Sallie said, worried.

Tsa'ni turned to look back at Sallie and asked, "My father has gone to Asheville with your grandfather?"

"Yes," Sallie replied. "But your mother should be at home. And Dimar's mother is visiting with her today."

"Where is my grandfather?" Tsa'ni asked.

"He went to his house in Bird-town," Sallie said.

"We are almost there," Dimar said to Tsa'ni. "Do you want to go to Sallie's house with us or do you want to go home to your house? I have to go to your house to tell my mother to wait for me, because I must ride back home with her. Then I will take Sallie and Mandie home."

"I will go to my house with you. I might want to ride with you to your house because I want to go back up the mountain, and you live up there not very far from where those men are digging right now," Tsa'ni said.

Mandie protested, "Tsa'ni, please don't go back up there by yourself to where those men are. They are angry with you now."

"That is not the first time they have been angry with me," Tsa'ni said. "I took their tools one day when they were sitting and eating."

"You took their tools? What did they do?" Mandie asked.

"They did not do anything," Tsa'ni said with a grin. "They were too anxious to find their tools. I would not tell them where I put them, but all the time the tools were just a few yards away, down by the creek. I was going to hide them a long way from there, but they found them before I could do that."

"I believe they are dangerous if they are lying about who they are," Dimar said.

"Yes, and, Tsa'ni, please do not incite their anger," Sallie said. "You should get some of the men to go with you and make them tell who they really are."

"Our men are not doing anything about the strangers," Tsa'ni reminded her.

Dimar pulled the cart into the yard of Tsa'ni's house. "There is my mother's cart, so she is still here," he said, jumping down. "I will tell her I am here, and then I will take you girls home." He hurried into the house.

Tsa'ni sat watching and didn't budge, not even to go into his own house.

"Are you not going inside to see your mother?" Mandie asked.

"I will when I come back," Tsa'ni said.

"Are we going to look for your grandfather's horse tomorrow?" Sallie asked.

"I said *I* would," Tsa'ni said, frowning at her.

Dimar returned, jumped onto the seat, and got the cart back out into the road. "I told my mother I would be back in a few minutes," he said. "They were eating supper."

"Oh, goodness! I hope Morning Star hasn't given up on us for supper," Mandie said with a gasp.

"She will wait for us," Sallie assured Mandie.

When Dimar pulled the cart into the yard at Uncle Ned's house, Morning Star was seated on the front stoop. The girls jumped down from the cart and Dimar and Tsa'ni took the cart down into the backyard. Dimar told the girls good-night as he and Tsa'ne walked back down the road to Tsa'ni's house.

As the girls approached the old woman, Morning Star spoke to Sallie in Cherokee. Sallie conversed with her as they entered the house.

Mandie put Snowball down and listened. She

sensed that something exciting had happened.

Sallie finally turned to translate the conversation for her. "My grandmother says the missionary was here just a little while ago. She was worried because he told her we should have been home before now."

"I'm sorry, Sallie. Please tell your grandmother I apologize for causing us to be so late," Mandie said, smiling at the old woman.

"That is not all," Sallie said. "The missionary would like you and me to bring the curtains and hang them in the schoolhouse tomorrow."

"But we are supposed to go with Tsa'ni tomorrow, if your grandmother gives us permission," Mandie said. "And Riley O'Neal doesn't speak Cherokee. How did he talk to your grandmother?"

"He had one of Drumgool's grandsons with him, and he knows how to speak both ways," Sallie explained. "Drumgool lives near the schoolhouse and his grandson will be one of the missionary's pupils."

"Well, what are we going to do about tomorrow?" Mandie asked.

Sallie glanced out the doorway and said, "Dimar and Tsa'ni have already gone. We can decide after we eat. My grandmother has the food waiting for us."

Mandie followed Sallie to the wash basin on the shelf and cleaned up.

Morning Star was busily putting the food on the table. Whatever she had cooked smelled delicious.

As they silently ate their supper, Mandie thought about the next day. She really did want to help out with the Cherokee schoolhouse but, on the other hand, she was anxious to solve the mystery about the strange men who were digging up the mountain.

Time was flying and she would soon have to return home in order to get ready for school in Asheville. She wondered, *How can I work out a solution and combine these two things?*

As Morning Star passed the bean bread, Mandie looked at Sallie and said, "Maybe Riley O'Neal would want to go with us to see the strange men."

"Remember, my grandfather told us not to go near the men, Mandie," Sallie reminded her. "Of course, it was accidental that we saw them today. And we could go back up the mountain with Dimar and Tsa'ni tomorrow, but we should not really be looking just for those men. I thought we could look for your uncle Wirt's horse."

Mandie looked at her again and said, "And if we run across the strange men while we're looking for Uncle Wirt's horse, then it would be accidental again."

"That is correct," Sallie said with a smile.

"Then maybe Mr. O'Neal would like to help us look for Uncle Wirt's horse," Mandie said. "We could go by there in the morning and find out."

"And take the green curtains for the schoolhouse, too," Sallie added.

Mandie figured it would only take a few minutes to hang the curtains in the schoolhouse, and then maybe the missionary would agree to go with them. *After all,* she thought, *he knew Uncle Wirt's horse was missing, and he was also interested in the talk about the strange men digging up the mountain.*

Chapter 9 / Digging Deep, Deep, Deep

Mandie and Sallie were already awake when the rooster crowed the next morning. They had gone to bed early the night before because they were worn out from lack of sleep. Uncle Ned had not come home from Asheville, and Morning Star had told the girls he and Jessan would probably stay two or three nights away from home while they sold their merchandise.

Snowball stood up on the bed and stretched. Then he jumped down, began meowing, and managed to move the partly open door with his paw in order to slip through.

Mandie watched him and smiled. "He smells food," she said as she, too, bounced out of bed. "And I think I smell coffee." She grabbed her clothes to get dressed.

Sallie followed. "My grandmother is getting

breakfast ready," she told Mandie as she pulled on her skirt.

"And do you remember who is supposed to be here this morning?" Mandie asked.

"Dimar will be here. I am not sure about Tsa'ni," Sallie said. "He may have stayed up on the mountain." She stepped into her moccasins.

"Dimar will be here to go with us to look for Uncle Wirt's horse, and Mr. O'Neal wants us to hang the curtains in the schoolhouse," Mandie reminded her. "So what do we do? Take Dimar with us to the schoolhouse and then ask Riley O'Neal to go with us to hunt for the horse?"

Sallie thought for a moment and then said, "I will have to ask my grandmother if it is all right to do that."

"What if Tsa'ni actually shows up this morning?" Mandie asked as she brushed her blond hair. "He said he would go look for the horse today, but he also told Dimar last night that he might want a ride back up the mountain. He is so wishy-washy about everything."

"If Tsa'ni comes here this morning we will take him to the schoolhouse and then to lock for the horse," Sallie said. She took her shell necklace from its nail on the wall, placed it over her head, and adjusted it around her slender neck.

"I can't imagine Tsa'ni agreeing to go to the schoolhouse after he protested so much about it being built," Mandie said. "But we will see. Ready?"

"Yes, ready," Sallie said.

The girls went down the ladder into the kitchen below. Morning Star had food cooking over the fire in the fireplace and steam was rising from the coffee kettle. She greeted them as they went to the water basin to wash their faces and hands.

"Eat," the old woman said with a big smile. She motioned to the table.

Mandie turned from drying her face and hands and walked over to hug the old Indian woman. "Love," she told Morning Star as she squeezed her hard.

"Love," Morning Star replied. Then pushing Mandie back to look into her face, the woman smiled and said, "Jim Shaw papoose."

Mandie instantly hugged her again as she said excitedly, "Morning Star, you are learning more and more English. I love you."

Morning Star stepped away from Mandie and said, "Jim Shaw papoose, eat." Then she grinned real big.

"Eat," Mandie agreed, blowing a kiss to Morning Star as she went to the table and sat down.

Sallie had been watching and listening. She sat down next to Mandie and said, "My grandmother has learned a lot of English since you started coming to see us. She never wanted to learn English before."

"But Uncle Ned said he and Morning Star lived with my father and Uncle John in Franklin when they were young boys. Did she not learn any English then? How did she communicate with my family?" Mandie asked as Morning Star placed a bowl of hot food in front of her.

"You forget, Mandie. Your father and your uncle John had a Cherokee mother from whom they learned Cherokee," Sallie reminded her. Her grandmother set a bowl before her and then the old woman took a bowl for herself and sat down across the table from the girls.

Mandie looked at Sallie and asked, "Do you mean my father could speak Cherokee?"

"Yes," Sallie said. "And of course your uncle John speaks the language."

"I've heard Uncle John talking to our Cherokee people in their language, but I never realized my father could speak it, too," Mandie said, with a distant look in her blue eyes as she remembered her father, who was always so kind and loving to everyone. She blinked back a tear.

"Eat," Morning Star told the girls as she started eating.

Mandie and Sallie hurriedly started in on the delicious mush in front of them. Mandie was quite sure the old woman had flavored it with ham gravy. She knew the Cherokee people were very thrifty with their food and would use and reuse anything they cooked until it was gone or too old to eat.

"This is good, Morning Star," Mandie told the woman.

"Good," the old woman said.

Mandie heard the sound of a horse coming into the yard and she leaned back to see out the open door. Dimar was already off his horse and tying it up.

"Dimar is here. Will you ask your grandmother if we can go look for Uncle Wirt's horse after we hang the curtains in the schoolhouse?" Mandie quickly asked Sallie.

Sallie spoke to her grandmother, and Morning Star replied, looking from one girl to the other as she spoke.

Mandie held her breath because Morning Star's reply didn't sound too pleased with whatever Sallie had asked her. Dimar came through the doorway and Morning Star immediately jumped up from the table, speaking to the boy in Cherokee as she hurried to the fireplace and filled another bowl with mush.

Dimar looked at the puzzled expression on Mandie's face and explained, "She just asked me to eat. That is all." He smiled as he stepped over the bench on the other side of the table and sat down in front of the girls.

Morning Star placed the bowl of mush in front of him and sat back down to finish her breakfast.

Sallie looked at Dimar and then at Mandie as she said, "My grandmother says we may go with Dimar to look for your uncle Wirt's horse, but that we must do whatever the missionary needs to be done *first*, and that we must be home in time to eat at noon."

"I'm glad she agreed to let us go," Mandie said, smiling at Morning Star. Turning to Dimar, Mandie asked, "Is Tsa'ni coming with us today?"

"I have not seen him since he went up the mountain with me and my mother last night when we went home," Dimar said. "What is it you have to do for the missionary?"

"We don't know," Mandie said as she explained that Mr. O'Neal had been out to see Morning Star while they were gone yesterday. "I know he wants us to hang the curtains we made, but I don't know what else. So we have to go to see him before we can do anything else."

"That is fine. I will help with whatever he needs done," Dimar replied as he ate the mush.

"This is good, isn't it?" Mandie said, watching him spoon away the food.

"It is good, but it is also the second time I have eaten this morning. My mother insisted I eat before

I left, and now this," Dimar said with a laugh.

"You will grow to be a fine, tall young man," Sallie assured him with a smile. "You will be big and strong like your father."

Dimar laughed and said, "I am almost as big as my father now, and I am fifteen years old. Therefore, I am almost grown."

"I suppose Tsa'ni is long gone in search of the two strangers," Mandie said as she finished her mush. "I doubt that he would really help us look for Uncle Wirt's horse anyway. You know, I wouldn't know his horse if I saw it. I don't remember seeing it when I've visited here before."

Dimar smiled and said, "Do not worry about that. I will recognize it."

Sallie finished her food and said, "As soon as we help my grandmother clear the table we will be ready to go." She stood up and reached for the dirty bowls.

Morning Star started trying to tell her something in Cherokee, but she paused, looked at Mandie, and then pointed to the door. "Go. Now. Eat—" she couldn't find the English word so she pointed straight up and squinted her black eyes.

Mandie understood that Morning Star meant "noontime." She stood up, smiled at Morning Star, and said, "We will be back to eat at noontime."

Morning Star grinned and said, "Noon, Noon, Eat."

"We must go now," Sallie said, rising from the table. So we will be back in time to eat at noon. My grandmother does not want us to help clear the table."

Snowball had been fed from a dish on the hearth while Morning Star was cooking. He had curled up to sleep, but now he rose, stretched, yawned, and came running to his mistress.

"Snowball, I suppose I'll have to take you," Mandie said, getting his red leash from a nail by the back door, where she had put it last night. He followed her and stood still for her to fasten the leash to his collar. Then Mandie picked him up.

Dimar went out the door and Sallie explained, "My grandmother told him to harness up the pony and cart. We will ride, which will be faster than walking."

"And we can always leave the cart on the road and walk through woods and pastures where there aren't any roads," Mandie said. "Please don't let Dimar take the cart up such rough places as Uncle Wirt did. We might have an accident again."

"Dimar will not take us on unsafe pathways. He is always careful about that. Your uncle Wirt was worried, tired, and in such a big hurry—and it was very dark—he did not realize how bad the trails were," Sallie explained.

The girls bid Morning Star goodbye and went outside as Dimar brought the cart around to the front.

Suddenly Mandie put her hand on Sallie's arm to stop her. "We're forgetting the curtains," Mandie said, laughing.

"Go ahead and get in the cart with Snowball. I will get them," Sallie said. She ran back inside the house.

Mandie climbed up on the seat of the cart and waited with Dimar. Sallie came hurrying back with her arms full of green curtains. Dimar took them and placed them on the bed of the wagon so they wouldn't wrinkle.

"That would have been silly to go all the way to the schoolhouse and then remember that we had forgotten the curtains, wouldn't it?" Mandie said with a laugh as the three left in the cart.

"We would have had to come back and get them, and we certainly would not have had time for anything else before the noon meal that way," Sallie agreed.

Dimar guided the cart on the road straight to the schoolhouse as the three young people talked.

"I will select a place for the festival while we are at the schoolhouse," Dimar said. "Our people are really excited about this."

"I sure hope they're not disappointed," Mandie said. She planned to tell about the beginning of her journey and then say a little about what each country was like. She was not positive that all of the older Cherokee people would even know where these foreign lands were.

"They will not be disappointed, Mandie," Sallie assured her as Dimar brought the cart into the schoolhouse yard.

The girls jumped down, and Dimar reached for the curtains. "I will bring these inside for you," he said, picking up the green material Mandie and Sallie had made into curtains.

When they opened the door of the schoolhouse, they found Riley O'Neal seated at a table which was covered with books and papers. He rose to welcome them.

"I am glad you could come. Dimar, I suppose these two girls got you into this. Please put the curtains over here," the missionary said, and he pointed to a long wooden bench nearby.

Dimar smiled as he glanced at the girls and said,

"They have caused me to come here, but I am always glad to help with the school. Is there anything I can do?"

Riley O'Neal looked at him and asked, "Do you, by any chance, know how to hang curtains? I'll have to admit that was not part of my education. So unless you or the girls know how this is accomplished, I'd say we're in bad shape." He grinned, and his blue eyes folded into wrinkles.

"Yes, I know how this is done. I have done this for my mother," Dimar replied.

"I also know how," Mandie added.

"And so do I," Sallie said.

"Then would you all please educate the schoolmaster in the art of hanging curtains?" Riley O'Neal asked, still laughing.

"I suppose you have a hammer," Mandie began.

"And some nails," Sallie added.

"You also need rods or heavy twine to hold them up," Dimar explained.

Mandie glanced at the tops of the windows and exclaimed, "Someone has already made rods. See, up there!"

The others looked up. There were thin rods cut from small limbs, attached above each window.

"Dimar, if you can reach the rods and take them down, Sallie and I will run them through the top hems of the curtains. Then you can put the curtains up," Mandie said. Looking at Riley O'Neal she explained, "You see, there's nothing to it."

"Yes, I see," the missionary said.

Dimar took down the rods. The girls pushed the rods through the top hems of the green curtains, then Dimar put the rods back up and shook out the folds of the material.

As soon as the task was completed, everyone stood back to admire the green curtains. The benches already had the matching green cushions.

"You girls did a very good job," Riley O'Neal told them.

"Now, what else did you have for us to do?" Mandie asked, glancing at her friends and then at Mr. O'Neal.

"Why, nothing that I know of. We're ready to open the school now, I believe," the missionary said.

Mandie quickly asked, "Then if you don't have anything for us to do, would you like to go with us to look for Uncle Wirt's horse? It hasn't been found yet."

"I certainly hope no one has stolen it. Has Tsa'ni ever come home?" Mr. O'Neal asked.

"We found him yesterday," Mandie said, and she told him what had transpired after meeting up with Tsa'ni.

Riley O'Neal listened and then said, "I really would like to see those strange men. They are *not* telling the truth. One does not go around digging holes all over the place to survey for a map."

"That's what we thought," Mandie said with a smile. "So they must be some kind of outlaws or something like that, wouldn't you think?"

"I have no idea, but they certainly sound like strange people," Riley said. He looked at Dimar and asked, "Have the Cherokee people decided what to do about these men?"

"No, but we plan to have a discussion among our people soon, maybe at the festival we are having for Mandie to tell us about her European journey," Dimar replied. "We have decided to pick a spot near here to have it. We will meet at night around a big fire outdoors."

Riley looked at Mandie and said, "I'm so glad you are going to share your travels with the Cherokee people. I will also be there, that's for sure."

Mandie felt her face go red. She wasn't particularly at ease with Mr. O'Neal, and she had hoped he wouldn't come to the festival. She felt as though he had been educated so far beyond her that he might be critical.

"I just plan to talk, that's all," Mandie said, looking up at Dimar. "Want to go outside now and pick the spot? Then we could go look for Uncle Wirt's horse."

"Will you be coming with us to search for the horse?" Sallie asked the missionary.

"No, I am sorry, but I have lots of paperwork to do to get ready for the school opening," Riley said. "But just in case you run across those strangers again, please come and tell me about them."

"We will," Sallie promised.

The three young people left the schoolhouse and walked around the surrounding area looking for the best place for their festival. They chose an open area within sight of the schoolhouse.

"This place is large enough for all our people," Dimar told the girls as they walked across the site. "I will get the wood and set up the fire, and you will need something a little higher up to sit or stand on so everyone can see you, Mandie."

Mandie was beginning to get nervous about the whole idea. She didn't like to be the focus of a crowd unless it was absolutely necessary, like the time she had spoken at the council house about the gold that had been found. The gold belonged to the Cherokee people, and she had to talk to them about that.

"I can build a small platform out of some boards. It would only take a few minutes to do this," Dimar said as he glanced at Mandie while the three of them surveyed the spot.

Mandie shrugged her shoulders as she held on to Snowball's leash and said, "Whatever you think."

As Mandie looked across the open space, Tsa'ni suddenly came out of the bushes on the other side. "Tsa'ni!" she exclaimed.

Dimar and Sallie were silent as the other Indian boy hurried toward them.

"The white men are digging deep, deep, deep, on the other side of the ridge there," he said, pointing back toward the direction from which he had come.

Mandie could see a high ridge beyond the trees.

"On sacred ground?" Dimar quickly asked.

Tsa'ni nodded, "Yes, on our ancestors' ground."

"Oh, no, they must not do that," Sallie said with a shocked expression.

Mandie looked from one to the other and then asked, "What is so special about the place where they are digging?"

Tsa'ni sighed and frowned as he replied curtly, "Just like a white girl not to understand. The sacred ground is the burial place of our ancestors."

Then Mandie was really shocked. How dare anyone dig in such a place! "What can we do about it?" Mandie asked.

"We will stop them," Dimar said firmly.

"I have sent out a call for a powwow immediately," Tsa'ni told him.

"And my grandfather and your father, Tsa'ni,

are still in Asheville," Sallie said, worried.

"My grandfather will speak, I am sure," Tsa'ni said. "He has seen the men digging in other places. He knows what they look like and how they are acting."

"Yes, I am sure Uncle Wirt will speak to the people," Mandie agreed. "Where are you going, Tsa'ni?"

"I am helping spread the message," Tsa'ni told her. Then frowning, he added, "We have our own message line, from man to man, all across the mountain. Have you forgotten?"

"No, I remember all about that. What can we do?" Mandie asked.

"Go back to Deep Creek and tell the people to meet at the council house as fast as they can get there. This is urgent. It cannot wait until sundown," Tsa'ni said. He was gone in a flash through the bushes behind the schoolhouse.

"We must go back and tell the missionary first," Dimar said to the girls as they all walked back toward the schoolhouse.

When the three entered the schoolroom again, the missionary was back at work at the table. He looked up, puzzled to see them so soon.

"Back already?" he asked as he stood up.

"We have come to tell you that we just saw Tsa'ni in the yard out there," Dimar said. "He has found the strangers digging in our sacred ground and is sending the message for all Cherokee people to go to the council house immediately for a pow-wow. You will be welcome to go with us, but white people are not allowed to go inside during the meeting, but you could wait outside."

"Oh, my goodness!" Riley O'Neal said with

great concern. "This could be a dangerous situation, couldn't it?"

"Yes, the Cherokee people may fight," Dimar replied. "We must hurry back to Deep Creek to let the people there know about this."

"You know where the council house is," Mandie said as they turned to leave.

"If you wish to go, you should get there immediately. The meeting will be held very soon," Sallie said to the missionary.

"Oh, yes, I will be there. As soon as I can hitch up my horse and wagon," the missionary replied. "I will look for you all there."

The three young people lost no time getting back to Deep Creek. Dimar expertly handled the cart even though they drove fast. They were soon pulling into Uncle Ned's yard.

Just as Dimar was about to tie the reins to the fence, Mandie had a horrible thought. Turning to her friends she said, "What if this is all a trick Tsa'ni is playing on his people?"

Dimar and Sallie looked at her, surprised.

"And if we participate, we will also be responsible for a false alarm," Dimar added slowly.

"And this could cause a lot of trouble," Sallie added.

Morning Star came to the doorway to see who was in her yard.

"Not eat now," she called to them.

Sallie ran to her and explained quickly in their language what was going on. Dimar listened and added a word or two. Mandie was dying of curiosity because she couldn't understand what they were saying.

Morning Star wiped her brow with the back of

her hand and shook her head. She looked puzzled and worried.

"My grandmother does not know what we should do, and my grandfather is not here," Sallie explained.

"We can't take a chance on this. If Tsa'ni is telling the truth and we don't help notify the people, it would be bad for us," Mandie said. "Why don't we spread the message but be sure to let people know it was Tsa'ni who started this?"

"That is what we should do," Dimar agreed.

"Yes," Sallie added. She spoke to her grandmother and told her what they would do. Morning Star smiled and nodded her head in affirmation.

Thus it was settled.

Chapter 10 / Sallie Disappears

Dimar drove the cart, and Mandie and Sallie went with him all over Deep Creek and the surrounding area to spread the news. Mandie couldn't do much herself because she didn't speak Cherokee, and most of the Cherokee people did not speak English. Therefore, Dimar and Sallie had to do the talking.

Sometimes Mandie could understand, because if the people did know English, Sallie or Dimar would talk to them in English so Mandie could know what was being said.

"We are carrying a message from Tsa'ni, son of Jessan, and grandson of Wirt Pindar," Dimar would repeat. "The strange men who have been digging all over the mountain are now digging in our sacred ground. All the Cherokee people must come at once to the council house to decide what should be done. Please tell this to everyone you see."

Mandie noticed that the Cherokee people had

136

different reactions to this message. Some showed extreme anger. Others seemed afraid. Some were speechless with shock. But every single person who heard the message was moved emotionally in some way.

Before they were finished, Dimar's mother, Jerusha, had arrived at Jessan's house to go with Meli to the powwow. Morning Star had also joined Meli.

The three young people stayed together and went on in the cart to the council house.

"Seems like every time I visit my Cherokee kinpeople we have to go to the council house for something," Mandie remarked along the way.

"You do not like going to the council house?" Sallie asked.

"Oh, yes, I love going there. It's the heart and soul of the Cherokee people," Mandie replied over the noise of the cart.

"We make lots and lots of decisions for our people at the council house powwows," Dimar told her.

Mandie still had Snowball with her. Now she wondered what she would do with him while she was in the meeting. Just as the seven-sided, dome-shaped council house came into view, she spotted Riley O'Neal sitting in his wagon nearby.

"Dimar, I need to stop and speak to Mr. O'Neal," Mandie told her friend. "I want to ask him if he'll hold on to Snowball for me since he has to wait outside."

"I am sure he will," Dimar said as he pulled on the reins and the pony stopped the cart beside the missionary's wagon.

Mandie stood up in the cart and held Snowball out to Riley O'Neal. "Would you please keep Snowball for me while I go inside?" she asked.

"Of course," he said, jumping down from his wagon to walk over and reach up for the cat. "I'll be right here when you come out."

Snowball didn't much like the idea of being transferred to someone else. He squirmed to get down, but Riley O'Neal firmly held Snowball's feet and the cat gave up as the missionary returned to the seat in his wagon.

Dimar had to drive on down a little distance before he could find a place to park the cart. Then the three of them stepped down from the cart and hurried to the council house.

Mandie was always fascinated with the building. There were bleachers inside to sit on. Huge log poles held up the dome-shaped, thatched roof, and the symbols of the clans adorned the posts. The place of the sacred fire was directly ahead as they entered. Behind the fire sat several men with stacks of papers and books.

Mandie looked around. The place was almost full. She followed Dimar and Sallie to seats on the top row of bleachers. From there she could see everyone. But she couldn't find Tsa'ni in the crowd.

"I don't see Tsa'ni," she whispered to Sallie and Dimar.

Her friends looked over the crowd.

"I do not see him either," Sallie said.

"Neither do I," said Dimar. "I do hope he comes to this meeting. It will be bad if he does not."

The three continued watching for the other Indian boy, but he didn't seem to be in the crowd.

"I'm afraid we've been tricked," Mandie said under her breath as the drumbeat began to call the meeting to order.

Then suddenly Mandie saw movement out of the

corner of her eye. She turned and saw Tsa'ni step up to a seat on the bleachers, and Uncle Wirt was with him. She called her friends' attention to them.

"Thank goodness, Tsa'ni must have been telling the truth," Mandie whispered.

"Yes," Sallie agreed.

Mandie noticed that Uncle Wirt continued on into the center of the meetinghouse and sat next to the men behind the fire, which meant that he would speak. She looked back at Tsa'ni and found him looking at her, but he quickly glanced away.

After the drums stopped, the man in the center behind the fire stood up and began speaking in Cherokee. Mandie looked anxiously at Dimar and Sallie. Dimar began translating in a whisper.

"He is saying that Tsa'ni, son of Jessan, grand-son of Wirt Pindar, has reported that two strange men are digging in our sacred ground and that this meeting is called to make a decision about what to do. Mr. Wirt Pindar will talk," Dimar explained.

Uncle Wirt stood up, raised his arms, and looked upward. The people immediately did likewise. Mandie knew he was saying a prayer. Dimar, standing next to Mandie, whispered the translation under his breath. Uncle Wirt was asking God to help his people do the right thing about the strangers.

When the prayer ended, the people sat down and Uncle Wirt began his speech. Mandie's heart went out to him as he stood there, looking so old and humble. She clasped her hands tightly in her lap.

"He is telling our people what the strangers have been doing: digging everywhere, telling us that they were government men making a survey for a map—which he says was not true," Dimar whispered to

Mandie. "So far, our people have not bothered the men, but now we must take action. We cannot let them disturb the spirits of our ancestors by digging in the burial mounds. And he says a group of our elder men will talk to the strangers and ask them to leave—"

Dimar was interrupted in his translation by the sudden yelling and stomping that rose from the audience. People began wildly swinging their arms around, jumping up and down, and screaming so loudly that Mandie covered her ears.

"What are they saying?" Mandie asked Dimar as she got close to his ear.

"Fight! Fight! Run white men off our land!" Dimar had to lean against Mandie's ear to make himself heard.

Mandie's heart did flip-flops. She didn't want any fighting. That would mean bloodshed and possible deaths. There were other ways to settle this. Before Mandie realized what she was doing, she had run to Uncle Wirt's side and was calling for the people to listen to her. Uncle Wirt put his arm around her shoulders and said into her ear, "Do not hear Papoose."

Mandie saw the drums sitting idle near where she was standing. She quickly stepped off the small platform, ran to pick up a drumstick lying there, and began pounding on a drum with it. This shocked the crowd into silence. The Cherokee people stared at her in surprise.

"I am sorry I had to do this," Mandie began, and she turned to see Dimar and Sallie by her side. Dimar began translating what she was saying. "We should not go into battle over this." This brought a loud roar from the people and Dimar said something that brought silence.

Please, God, tell me what to say, Mandie silently prayed. *We can't fight. These white men are outlaws, but they will be killed and no telling how many Cherokee people will also wind up dead. Please put the right words into my mouth.*

Everyone was staring at Mandie, waiting to see what she would say or do.

Dimar whispered, "Talk now while they are silent. Now. Hurry."

"As you all know, I am part of you people. My grandmother was a full-blooded Cherokee, and the Cherokee blood is in my veins," Mandie said. "But I am also white."

The crowd began yelling and stomping again. But Uncle Wirt held up his hand and yelled out a few words. The crowd became silent.

"It is a sin to kill. That's one of the Ten Commandments: 'Thou shalt not kill.' And I know you all know what the Ten Commandments are," she continued.

Murmurs ran through the crowd.

"You know, as well as I do, if we begin a battle with these white men they will be killed because they are outnumbered, but some of our Cherokee people may also be killed, because those men are bound to have guns and ammunition."

Mandie saw a few heads bow and she knew they had understood her point.

"Let's go talk to these men. Let my uncle Wirt take a group of Cherokee men to search these men out. Make them understand that this is our land. Make them understand that the Cherokee people believe they are disturbing the spirits of our ancestors in the sacred burial ground. They should understand this. Even graves of white people are not allowed to be dug into like this," Mandie continued. She paused and looked around the council house. She knew many of the Cherokee people, and all of them knew her.

Suddenly there was a loud yell from the back of the bleachers. Mandie looked in that direction and saw Tsa'ni standing up and waving his arms as he screamed in Cherokee.

Dimar translated for Mandie, "He is telling the people to fight, that that is the only way."

Mandie began shouting to make herself heard over Tsa'ni's yells. "Let us try talking to the strangers first," she begged. "And if that doesn't work, then we will have another meeting to decide what to do next. Let's don't rush into a bloody battle."

Tsa'ni continued yelling, but suddenly the crowd began talking loudly in Cherokee among themselves. Mandie felt Uncle Wirt's arm tighten around her shoulders. She looked up at him, and when she saw his big smile, she knew she had succeeded. *Thank you, God, thank you,* she silently prayed.

Someone beat on the drums and the crowd became quiet. Then Uncle Wirt began speaking again. Several men in the crowd stepped forward. Dimar whispered that her uncle was asking for volunteers to go talk to the men with him.

Uncle Wirt spoke again with a laugh, and Dimar smiled and translated, "He is saying, 'Just a few men. We do not need every man to go. Others can go later if these men cannot convince the white men to leave.'"

Mandie looked in the direction where Tsa'ni had been standing. There was no sign of him in the crowd. He was going to be awfully angry with her for what he would call meddling in the Cherokees' business. But she was not worried about that. She felt she had done the right thing.

The crowd began moving out of the council house. Mandie's knees suddenly became weak and she sat down on the bleacher behind her. She drew a deep breath as she realized how bold she had been. Uncle Ned had always taught her to think first. She felt that she *had* thought about the situation first, but she had felt almost automatically propelled to the platform in front of these people. Now she felt weak and shy. Dimar and Sallie sat beside her, and Uncle Wirt began talking to the men who had come forward.

"That was a good thing you did for our people," Dimar told her, pride showing on his face as he looked into her blue eyes.

"Yes, you kept our people from making a big mistake," Sallie agreed.

"But now, I have to admit, I'm scared," Mandie said in a shaky voice. "I don't know whether I have the strength to walk out of this place."

Dimar stood up, offered his hand, and said, "Come on. We will go with you to find Snowball and to tell the missionary what the outcome of the meeting was."

Mandie took his hand and stood up. "I imagine Riley O'Neal *will* be anxious to find out what happened," she said with new strength. "And Snowball may be giving him trouble by now. Let's go."

The three young people managed to work their way through the crowd and found Riley O'Neal standing outside the doorway, with Snowball asleep in his arms.

Before they could speak, Riley O'Neal said, "I heard all the ruckus and was afraid something bad had happened."

Mandie laughed and said, "That's the way the Cherokee people react to anything they don't like. They are awfully emotional when it comes to protecting their people and their property."

Dimar smiled at her and said to the missionary, "What really happened was that Mandie talked the people out of going into battle, for the time being at least."

"Good for you," Riley said as Mandie reached for her cat.

Snowball opened his blue eyes, stretched, and tried to jump down. Mandie let him down on his leash.

"I expect Tsa'ni will try stirring something up, because he wanted nothing but to go into battle with those white men," Mandie explained.

Uncle Wirt and his group of men pushed their way through the crowd. He stopped to speak with Mandie. "We go now," he said with a big smile.

"Please, be careful, Uncle Wirt," Mandie said as she looked up at him. "And watch out for Tsa'ni, I know he's your grandson, but he doesn't like what we are doing."

Uncle Wirt shrugged and said, "We watch." He went on down the road with the other men.

Mandie looked at her friends and said, "Why don't we go just near enough to the digging to see what happens?"

Sallie looked at her with round eyes. "But, Mandie, those strangers might not agree to what our men are asking, and they may become angry and do something dangerous."

Mandie gasped and said, "I hope I'm not sending Uncle Wirt and the other men into trouble. I hadn't thought about that."

"Your uncle Wirt is a man of honor," Dimar said. "The meeting with the white men will not be angry, but he will be firm."

"Oh, but, Dimar, I am worried about this," Mandie said. "Would you please take us to the place where they are digging? I won't go near enough for anyone to see me, I promise. Please."

Dimar looked at her, and so did Riley O'Neal. Sallie sighed.

"I will go with you if you wish," the missionary told Dimar. "It should be safe enough if the strangers don't see us. I'd really like to take a look at them myself."

Mandie looked at Dimar and then at Sallie.

"All right," Dimar finally agreed, "But I will hold you to your word, Mandie, that you will not go near the strangers."

"I will hold Snowball and stay in the cart down on the road," Sallie said.

"Leave your wagon here," Dimar told the missionary. "We will all go in the cart."

"Thanks, everybody," Mandie said, smiling as the group hurried down the road to the parked cart.

Mandie looked around, but couldn't see Uncle Wirt and the men with him anywhere near, so they must have rushed right out to the place where the men were digging. She hoped the meeting wouldn't be over by the time they got there.

The girls volunteered to sit in the bed of the wagon and allow Riley O'Neal to have the seat beside Dimar. As they traveled hastily down the road, Dimar explained to the missionary what had transpired in the council house. Riley looked back at Mandie several times with a proud smile. It made her feel like she was blushing.

"I wonder what my grandfather will say when he returns and finds we had a meeting about the strangers," Sallie remarked, as Snowball at the end of his leash darted from one girl to the other. Sallie rubbed his fur.

"I think he would have done the same thing," Mandie said. "He has always told me to think before I do anything in a rush. And the way we are doing this is like thinking first. We go slow at first, and if that works, then everything will be all right. If it doesn't work, then we will have to do something stronger about it."

"Yes, I understand what you mean," Sallie agreed.

Before long, Dimar pulled the cart up beside the roadway and said, "Now we have to walk." He jumped down to help Mandie from the cart.

Riley O'Neal stepped down beside her. He looked at Sallie, who was still sitting in the wagon, and asked, "Are you coming with us?"

"No, I will stay here and keep Snowball so he cannot cause any trouble," Sallie said with a laugh as she rubbed Snowball's fur.

"We should not be gone long," Dimar told Sallie. "Please do not leave the cart."

"I will be sure to stay right here," Sallie promised.

Dimar led the way, while Mandie and Riley O'Neal followed him up a trail through the woods on the side of the mountain. Mandie lifted the hem of her long skirt to keep from becoming entangled in the underbrush. It was clear to Mandie that this trail was seldom used.

"We have to climb to the ridge and go over," Dimar explained as he walked on. "I will warn you before we get there so we can be quiet and not attract attention."

"We certainly don't want to attract any attention," Riley O'Neal agreed as he brought up the rear.

"I wonder if Tsa'ni came up here," Mandie said as she stepped over rough rocks protruding from the terrain.

"I would think he came straight here from the council house and probably got here before your uncle Wirt and the other men did," Dimar replied as he pushed back bushes along the way.

"Oh, I hope he didn't get here first and cause trouble with the men," Mandie said with a gasp. "He could ruin everything for Uncle Wirt and the other men."

"Maybe he will just wait and watch," Riley said.

But at that very moment, Mandie knew something had gone wrong. She heard shouting and the sound of heavy boots running down the mountainside toward them. Dimar motioned quickly for Mandie and the missionary to get behind the bushes nearby. They all hid from the approaching voices.

The noise came closer, and Mandie's heart beat faster. Tsa'ni must have gone up there and caused trouble. Suddenly the sound was passing before them, and Mandie glimpsed the two strange men running down the mountainside with several Cherokee men chasing behind them.

"The cart!" Mandie said, gasping in fright.

"They are heading toward the cart, and Sallie is down there alone!"

Dimar quickly plunged down the hill after the men. Mandie and Riley O'Neal followed.

Mandie thought it seemed to take forever to get far enough down to see the cart on the road below, and when she finally did see it, her heart gave a lurch. She saw the strangers jump into the cart, shake the reins, and rush off. Snowball jumped from the wagon bed, but Sallie was nowhere in sight.

"Hurry! Hurry!" she cried, and Dimar plunged ahead.

The Cherokee men were standing in the roadway staring at the disappearing cart when Mandie finally got there. Snowball was hunched up in fright at the activity. Mandie snatched him up in her arms. She looked around and thought, *Where is Sallie?*

"Was Sallie in that cart?" Dimar quickly demanded from the nearest Cherokee man standing there.

The man shook his head. None of the men had seen her.

The men, along with Dimar, the missionary, and Mandie, quickly fanned out around the area to look for Sallie, making sure they stayed within sight of each other. Several men began calling out her name.

Mandie was searching the pathway when Uncle Wirt came down the hill and asked, "What happen?"

"Sallie is gone," Mandie tried to tell him. She knew he understood more English than he could speak. "She was in the cart before the men stole it. But we don't know if she was taken or not."

Uncle Wirt excitedly called the other Cherokee men. Then Dimar explained what had happened.

"If she was in the cart when the men took it, I could not see her," Dimar said.

"Maybe she got out when she saw them coming," Mandie suggested.

Uncle Wirt spoke loudly to two men in the group.

Dimar translated for Mandie and Riley O'Neal. "He is telling them to get their horses, which are hidden in the bushes across the road, and chase the cart. The other men came in a wagon which they have hidden on a trail off the road down that way." He pointed in the direction the cart had gone.

"Can we ride in the wagon?" Mandie asked Dimar.

"I am sure we can," Dimar said.

Uncle Wirt and several of the men began sending bird calls. Mandie knew they were calling on other Cherokee men to help in the search for Sallie.

Mandie felt this situation was all her fault. She should not have suggested coming out here, and she should not have left Sallie alone in the cart.

If Sallie had hidden anywhere nearby, Mandie was sure she would have shown up by now. Her blue eyes filled with tears as she worried about what happened.

Dimar looked at her and took her hand in his. He said, "Do not blame yourself. I am sure Sallie will be found and will be all right."

Riley O'Neal walked over to join Dimar and Mandie. The men were still searching the area.

Mandie squeezed Dimar's hand and, holding on to Snowball's leash, reached for the missionary's hand. She told him, "We have a special verse for times of trouble. No matter what has happened or is about to happen, whether it's danger, worry, or whatever, we join hands and quote the verse. It helps us remember God's protection over us.'' She recited the verse to him.

Riley smiled at her and said, ''Now let's all say it together.''

''What time I am afraid, I will put my trust in Thee,'' they said in unison.

Mandie released Riley's and Dimar's hands and wiped her blue eyes.

She picked up Snowball and said, ''Now it's all in God's hands. We don't have to worry anymore.''

Mandie just couldn't figure out where Sallie had gone, but she hoped her friend would be found soon. When Uncle Ned came home and heard about this, he was going to be awfully put out with her.

Chapter 11 / Send for Uncle Ned

Uncle Wirt sent the men after their wagon while he waited with the young people and Mr. O'Neal. He had agreed that they could ride in the wagon.

"Uncle Wirt, things got so noisy and happened so fast, all of a sudden, that we haven't even asked what happened to make the strangers run away like that," Mandie said.

Uncle Wirt looked at Dimar. Wirt didn't seem to understand exactly what Mandie meant. Dimar explained in Cherokee, and then the old man told them, "Tsa'ni hide, shoot arrow at strange men. Strange men see us, think we did shooting. They run, afraid."

"Tsa'ni!" Mandie exclaimed, "I knew he would do something, because he didn't get his way at the council house."

"Where is Tsa'ni?" Dimar asked.

"Go away," Uncle Wirt replied.

"Did anyone get hurt by Tsa'ni's arrows?" Riley asked.

Dimar had to translate that question, too. Uncle Wirt shook his head, "No, just afraid."

The two men who had gone for the wagon came hurrying up now to join them.

Uncle Wirt motioned for the young people and Riley O'Neal to get into the back. He sat on the seat by the two men. The driver snapped the reins and rushed the horses down the roadway.

"Where are we going?" Mandie asked Dimar. She noticed that they were going in the opposite direction from the one the strangers had taken with the cart.

"I am not positive, but I believe your uncle Wirt knows how to go around and cut back through on another road to get ahead of the strangers," Dimar said. "The road they took winds around and around and is much longer."

"If we are able to get ahead, what will happen when they meet up with us?" Riley asked.

"They will probably try to turn around or get out and run for the woods," Dimar said.

"Do you think they may have guns and will shoot at us?" Mandie asked, holding tight to Snowball as the wagon bounced along.

"No, your uncle Wirt will stop and leave us in a safe spot before a clash can happen," Dimar assured her.

"I wish I knew where to look for Sallie," Mandie said. "She must have gotten out of the cart before the men took off. But if she did, where did she go? If she was still around back there where we stopped the cart, she would know we were all searching for her. Oh, where can she be?'' Her voice quivered, and she blinked back tears.

"We will find her,'' Riley O'Neal reassured her. "Remember the verse we said. Put your trust in the Lord.''

Mandie could only nod her head. She was unable to speak, so great was her grief.

The driver suddenly swerved the wagon onto another road, and Mandie hugged Snowball in her arms as she, Dimar, and the missionary were thrown around in the wagon bed.

As the wagon straightened out, Dimar said, "I was right. Your uncle Wirt is going to cut them off.''

"Shouldn't the two men on horseback chasing the cart catch up with the strangers?'' Riley asked.

"Maybe,'' Dimar said. "They might not stop the cart, but just follow it to see where it is going.''

Mandie looked ahead and suddenly saw the cart approaching in the distance.

Suddenly the driver of the wagon halted the horses. Uncle Wirt looked at the three in the wagon bed and said, "Quick! Wait! Hide!'' He pointed to a thick stand of bushes on the right.

Dimar helped Mandie and Snowball down. Riley O'Neal held out his hand for her last step. The three scurried into the bushes as the wagon jerked forward and raced on down the road again.

"I hope no one gets hurt,'' Mandie said, peering through a small opening in the foliage. She could see the wagon and the cart driving straight at each other.

"They are slowing down,'' Riley O'Neal said as he stood behind Mandie.

She noticed the two men on horseback were still in pursuit of the strangers.

"If your uncle is able to talk to the strangers, no one will be hurt," Dimar told her as he watched.

"They're stopping," Mandie added as Snowball squirmed in her arms.

The driver of the Cherokees' wagon pulled it to a halt across the road. Uncle Wirt stepped down and waited for the strange men.

As the three watched from behind the bushes, they saw the strangers in the cart pull to a halt as they approached the wagon. The strange men looked scared.

Uncle Wirt was hard-of-hearing so he talked loudly all the time. This time he spoke so loudly that his voice carried back to Mandie and her friends.

"We talk!" he called to the two strangers as he walked toward them with the two men who had been with him in the wagon.

"Don't shoot any more arrows at us!" the big man called to Uncle Wirt.

"We not shoot arrows. Bad Cherokee boy shoot arrow. We talk," Uncle Wirt said as he continued toward the cart.

Mandie could see the strangers watching Uncle Wirt and his two men and then turn to watch the two men who rode up behind them on horseback. They were surrounded, and they were uncertain about what to do next.

Uncle Wirt hurried toward the cart and looked into the bed. "Where Papoose? What you do with Papoose?" he demanded angrily.

The two men with him stationed themselves on each side of the cart. None of the men were carrying bows or arrows, but Mandie knew their weapons were in the wagon.

"What are you talking about, old man?" the big

man demanded. "What papoose?"

"Sallie Sweetwater, granddaughter of Ned Sweetwater, wait in cart—and you take cart. Where is Papoose Sallie? Tell now!" Uncle Wirt balled up his fists and shook them at the men.

"There was nobody in the cart when we took it," the big man said, straightening up. "We ain't seen no papoose."

"You take Papoose and we will fight," Uncle Wirt told them. "We will fight, too, if you do not get off sacred ground of the Cherokee people. No more digging!"

"Fight all you want to, old man," the big man said. "We ain't got no gal with us, and we gonna dig all we want. Git out of the way!" He quickly snapped the reins of the cart and the pony shot forward, squeezing around the wagon blocking the road.

Mandie held her breath. Uncle Wirt barely got out of the way. The two men on horseback immediately raced forward after the cart. As Uncle Wirt hurried toward his wagon, the cart rushed past the bushes where the young people were hiding and out of their view.

Suddenly a loud crash broke through the air. "What happened?" Mandie asked, leaving her hideaway and racing into the road to see the cart. Dimar and Riley O'Neal followed. The cart was out of sight around the next curve.

Uncle Wirt and his two men, who had been standing in the road looking in the direction the cart had gone, jumped into the wagon and hurried after it.

"Let's go!" Mandie told her friends. She held on to Snowball with one arm, lifted her long skirts with the other, and ran down the road.

Dimar and the missionary caught up with her and the three ran around the bend in the road. There they saw what had happened. The cart had lost a wheel—the same wheel that had come off when Uncle Wirt had been driving it on the mountain. The two men who had been on horseback were working with the harness, trying to free the trapped pony.

"Oh, I hope the poor pony is not hurt," Mandie cried.

By the time Dimar, Mandie, and Riley O'Neal got to the cart, the men had freed the pony and tied him to a tree. He was not hurt. Uncle Wirt and his men were in the middle of the road talking loudly with angry voices. The strangers had escaped.

"Dimar, what is Uncle Wirt saying?" Mandie asked as they stood there watching the Cherokee men.

"He is angry that the men got away. He is also angry because we have not been able to find Sallie," Dimar translated. "He is telling the men to send the word throughout the mountain to capture the strangers and to look for Sallie."

"It shouldn't take long to capture the strangers, because the mountain and the hills are full of Cherokee people who will search," Riley O'Neal said.

"They will search for Sallie first," Dimar explained.

"If only we knew how to contact Tsa'ni, he always seems to know where the strangers are," Mandie said. "And I think the strangers are responsible for Sallie's disappearance."

"He will learn of this when the message is sent to all the Cherokee people," Dimar said.

The two men who had been on horseback were fixing the cart, trying to get the wheel back on. Uncle Wirt motioned to the young people to get into his wagon.

"In," he called to them, pointing toward the wagon.

As the three of them climbed into the bed of the wagon, Uncle Wirt and one of the men climbed onto the seat.

"The other man is not coming," Mandie said, pointing to the other man who had been riding in the wagon with them.

"It will take three men to finish the job with the cart: one to drive the cart and two to ride the horses," Dimar explained.

"Of course," Mandie agreed.

Uncle Wirt looked back at them and said, "Home now."

The other man called to the horses, and the wagon rushed on down the road.

Home? Mandie thought. *"Home" means Uncle Ned's house. What am I going to say to Morning Star about Sallie?* She worried so much she felt sick to her stomach.

When they arrived at Uncle Ned's house, Mandie removed Snowball's leash. He jumped down from the wagon and ran into the house.

Morning Star was sitting on the front stoop, and she rose to greet them. Mandie ran toward her and burst into tears. Morning Star put her arms around Mandie and spoke softly in Cherokee. Dimar and Riley O'Neal followed. Dimar told Morning Star in Cherokee what had happened.

Morning Star started telling Dimar something. She spoke louder and faster until she was almost shouting.

Dimar explained to Mandie and Riley, "She

wants us to send word to Sallie's grandfather to come home from Asheville immediately."

"Yes, we need Uncle Ned real bad," Mandie said, choking on a sob.

Uncle Wirt and the other man had tethered their horses in the yard, and Uncle Wirt came to speak to Morning Star. As he talked, he sounded angry and began shaking his fists in the air. Morning Star wrapped her arms around herself and cried. Then Uncle Wirt and the other man walked back to the wagon.

"They are going to start the call for the search," Dimar said as he quickly ran to the wagon to speak to Uncle Wirt. Mandie followed him. She knew he was probably asking to be included in the search party, and she wanted to join in.

"Please, Uncle Wirt, can I go help look for Sallie? Please? It's all my fault, and we've just got to find her," Mandie begged the old man.

Uncle Wirt didn't seem to understand everything Mandie said, but when Dimar translated for him, the old man looked down at Mandie and said, "Jim Shaw's papoose must stay here. May be trouble."

"Uncle Wirt, please let me go!" Mandie kept begging.

"Mandie, I am going. I'll do the best I can," Riley O'Neal told her.

Mandie and Dimar turned to look at the missionary. Mandie thought, *He can't understand the people. What can he do?*

"We are going by the road that leads to the council house, and you will be able to get your wagon that you left there," Dimar told Riley.

"Thanks, but I really do want to help," Riley insisted. He walked over to Uncle Wirt and made motions with his hands while he said, "I help find Sallie."

To Mandie's surprise, Uncle Wirt motioned for the missionary to get into the back of the wagon. Dimar hurried into the backyard and came back on his horse. Bending down to Mandie, he said, "I will keep in touch with you and let you know what happens."

Uncle Wirt pulled the wagon out onto the road, and Dimar quickly followed on his horse. Mandie turned back to look at Morning Star. The old woman held out her arms to Mandie, and Mandie ran to her embrace. Their tears mixed.

Mandie sat with Morning Star on the front stoop for several minutes. Then the woman rose and motioned for Mandie to follow her.

"Eat," Morning Star told her. She took bowls from a shelf and went to the pot over the fire in the fireplace to fill them.

Mandie went to the basin and splashed water on her swollen eyes and dried off.

"Sit," Morning Star said, pointing to the table. She carried a bowl of food and set it on the table as Mandie sat down. She went back and got another bowl for herself, then sat across from Mandie.

They spoke little because of the language barrier, but they could make each other understand with hand motions.

"Eat," Morning Star said sternly as Mandie sat looking at the bowl of hot stew. "Eat."

Mandie knew what the old woman was thinking. All grown people seemed to think that food was important in a time of crisis. Back home, Aunt Lou, Uncle John's housekeeper, always quoted an old saying that said a person couldn't think on an empty stomach.

With a big sigh, Mandie picked up the spoon and tasted the stew. She perked up as the delicious food found its way to her stomach. Maybe the old saying was true.

As soon as they had finished the stew, Morning Star poured two cups of strong, hot coffee. Coffee was another remedy for such times. Mandie picked up the cup with both hands and sipped the hot, dark liquid. It was good!

Morning Star was watching Mandie, and now she asked, "Good?"

Mandie nodded and said, "Good." She longed to talk to the old woman, but she knew Morning Star would only become confused because she couldn't understand English.

Suddenly Mandie realized there were voices in the yard outside—voices speaking English, voices that belonged to the strangers. Her heart pounded, and she glanced at Uncle Ned's rifle hanging over the doorway. She knew he kept it loaded, but she doubted she could reach it.

"Men," Morning Star said softly as she, too, glanced toward the doorway.

Mandie nodded. She quickly slid a stool over to one side of the open door, stood up on it, and managed to get Uncle Ned's rifle down. She stepped back and put it to her shoulder.

Morning Star looked at her in surprise but didn't say anything. A shadow fell across the floor from the doorway, and Mandie looked up to see the larger of the two strange men standing in the doorway looking inside.

"Don't move!" she yelled, and she pointed the

rifle at the man. She steeled herself for a possible shot. Just like all country people, Mandie's father had taught her to shoot a rifle. She was small for the big gun, but she knew how to use it.

"Well, if it ain't the little lady that runs around with them Cherokee people!" the man sneered at her from the doorway. "Better let me have that big gun, little lady. It's too big for the likes of you." He started to reach for it.

Mandie stiffened her legs and spoke angrily, "I know how to use this, mister! And if you don't leave, I'll show you that I do! Now get out of here!" The rifle was heavy, but she didn't waver.

"We only want a drink of water," the man said. "That's all." He smiled at her. "Now you wouldn't kill me with that thing, would you?"

"No, I wouldn't kill you. It's a sin to kill, but I will hurt you so you won't ever forget it if you don't leave now. I'm warning you. You'd better go while you can," Mandie said, squinting her blue eyes at the man.

Suddenly the man's expression changed to terror as he glanced behind her. Mandie quickly looked back. Tsa'ni was standing there with his bow stretched back and an arrow aimed squarely at the man. Mandie thought, *He must have come in the back door.*

When the boy saw that Mandie had seen him, he pulled the arrow from the bow and dropped it back into the quiver. He walked forward and reached for the gun. "Let me have that. I will fix this man for you," he said.

"No, Tsa'ni, just make him leave," Mandie said as Tsa'ni tried to take the rifle. She stepped back and then looked for the man. He was gone.

She relaxed for a moment, and Tsa'ni was able to take the rifle from her.

"I will follow him," Tsa'ni said. He hoisted the rifle to his shoulder and started toward the door.

Mandie laid a hand on his arm. "Tsa'ni, have you heard? Sallie is missing. We need to look for her."

Tsa'ni stopped in his tracks and looked straight at Mandie. "Sallie is missing? Our Sallie is missing?" he repeated. "Where did she go?" He dropped the rifle to his side.

Mandie quickly related what had happened. Tsa'ni turned and spoke in Cherokee to Morning Star, who had sat silently at the table during the whole incident. Morning Star's words were angry. Mandie had no way of knowing what the two were saying, but she watched them closely.

"I will go find Sallie," Tsa'ni said firmly. Before he left, he replaced the rifle over the doorway and straightened the arrows in his deerskin pouch.

Mandie hurried to catch him as he headed outside. "I am going with you," she told him. She didn't care what he said, she was determined that she was going along. As much trouble as Tsa'ni was always causing, this was one time Mandie had really been glad to see him. She would have hated having to fire Uncle Ned's rifle.

"Why?" Tsa'ni stopped to ask.

"Because it was partly my fault that this happened," Mandie said. "Besides, you don't know where we parked the cart. Therefore, you don't know where to look for her."

"But I know where the strange white men stay," Tsa'ni said. "I will make them tell me where Sallie is."

"Tsa'ni, we're not sure the strangers know anything about where Sallie is. She could have gotten out of the cart before they took it," Mandie told him.

"All right," Tsa'ni finally relented. "You show me where you stopped the cart."

"Please tell Morning Star what we're going to do. She can't understand me, you know," Mandie said as she glanced at the old woman still sitting by the table.

Tsa'ni stepped back into the room and spoke to Morning Star. She obviously didn't want Mandie to go. "Stay here," she insisted, coming to stand by the girl. "Stay."

"I'll be back soon, Morning Star," Mandie promised, and with a quick embrace she turned to follow Tsa'ni into the yard.

The two searched the barns quickly to be sure the strange men were gone, but there was no sign of anyone.

"I hope Morning Star will be safe while we're gone," Mandie said.

"I told her to go to my mother's house, and she said she would," Tsa'ni said as they walked across the road.

The two had gone a long distance into the woods and up the mountain before Mandie realized Snowball was following her. She heard his meow as they stopped to look around a clearing. He came running out of the bushes and began rubbing around her ankles.

"Snowball, how could you follow me at a time like this!" Mandie exclaimed. She picked him up. He didn't have his leash on, so she would have to carry him.

"That white cat always causes trouble," Tsa'ni

said angrily. "Send him back."

"Tsa'ni, he won't go back. Cats don't understand if you tell them to go home," Mandie replied. "I'll see that he behaves."

Tsa'ni pulled the end of the coil of rope hanging on his shoulder. He took a knife from his belt and cut off a short length of it. He handed it to Mandie and said, "Tie this on him."

Mandie looked at the thick rope and knew it would not thread through Snowball's collar. But then she noticed that it was unraveling. She quickly pulled out a thin strand and tied it to Snowball's collar as Tsa'ni watched. Then she set the cat down.

"Where are we going, Tsa'ni?" Mandie asked as they continued on.

"You will show me where the cart was stopped," Tsa'ni said, looking back at her.

"But, Tsa'ni, we didn't go this way. We went down the road with the cart," Mandie told him. She paused to look at him.

"This is a shortcut to the road," Tsa'ni said. "I know where the strangers were when my grandfather and the other men found them." He walked on.

Yes, he knew where they were. Mandie remembered that Tsa'ni had shot the arrow that had caused all this trouble. But she wasn't going to remind him of that. She was afraid he might just walk off and leave her, and she would never find the way back to Uncle Ned's house alone. She knew she would just have to trust him to help find Sallie.

Chapter 12 / Rescued!

Mandie followed Tsa'ni through woods, up hills, down through valleys, and into clearings. Sometimes she was able to walk by his side, but most of the time the trails that Tsa'ni hacked his way through were too narrow and she stayed behind him. She was wondering if he really knew where he was going, but she was aware of his temper and didn't dare question him. Right now she needed to find Sallie, and she believed she would with Tsa'ni's help.

As Mandie hurried alongside Tsa'ni through one of the clearings, she looked up at him and said, "You know, Tsa'ni, while the men were looking for your grandfather, my uncle Wirt, someone went to the schoolhouse and lit the missionary's lamp. Then when he came home, it was out and a fire had been lit in the fireplace."

Tsa'ni stopped and squinted his black eyes at her. He said, "I lit the lamp and put it out, and I lit the fire and left it going." He watched and waited for her reaction.

Mandie tried not to be too bold, but she said, "Tsa'ni, that is the missionary's private room in the schoolhouse."

"It is not," Tsa'ni said firmly. "The whole school building belongs to the Cherokee people. Nothing belongs to that missionary."

Mandie swallowed hard, thinking about what she should say. She did not want to start an argument. "Well, why did you light the lamp and then put it out, and then light the fire?" she asked.

"I lit the lamp so I could see," Tsa'ni said, speaking to her as though she were a child. "And I lit the fire so I could get warm. When I left, I put out the lamp. Do you understand?"

"Then you must have been around when we went looking for the missionary in his room," Mandie said.

"Yes, I heard you coming and I waited in the back-yard until you had left," Tsa'ni said. "Now, if you are finished asking questions, we will continue on."

"Yes, let's hurry and find Sallie. I'm worried about her," Mandie replied.

Tsa'ni kept moving through the woods, and Mandie followed. The sun began disappearing behind the tall mountain. Darkness came faster up there, and the air became chilly. Snowball snuggled in Mandie's arms, helping to keep her warm. Finally Mandie could only pick her way through the bushes by the dim light of the moon and she held her breath lest she trip.

Tsa'ni suddenly stopped in front of Mandie, nearly causing her to collide with him from behind. He breathed deeply and Mandie took a deep breath too. The smell of burning wood was in the air.

"Be quiet now," Tsa'ni told her, turning to face her. "Someone is nearby and they have a fire going. You stay here. I will see who it is. Do not follow me or make any noise."

Mandie nodded her head in silence and stood rooted to the ground as the boy silently disappeared through the bushes ahead. She felt positive they had finally found the strangers' camp, but would Sallie be with them?

In a few minutes, Tsa'ni reappeared in front of her. He motioned for silence and he took Mandie a short distance back the same way they had come.

Finally he stopped and whispered, "The strangers are there, and they have Sallie tied to a tree. They also have my grandfather's horse. Now here is what we will do. I will circle around to the other side and make a noise to draw their attention. Then I will throw my rope around the big man." He took his knife from his belt and held it out to Mandie. "You take my knife and cut the ropes to free Sallie."

Mandie's heart beat wildly. *The strangers have Sallie,* she thought. *And now I must put myself in danger to save her.* She took the knife.

"Can you do this?" Tsa'ni asked, looking straight into her blue eyes. "There will be no danger if you do exactly as I tell you. I will rope up the big man because the small man is a coward. He will not cause trouble. He will run away."

Mandie silently breathed her verse, *What time I am afraid, I will put my trust in Thee.* She replied, "I can do it, Tsa'ni. Please be careful."

Tsa'ni gave her a long look in the moonlight

and disappeared silently into the bushes again.
Mandie crept forward until she could see the fire
going in a small clearing. The two men were sitting
beside it and Sallie was tied to a tree nearby. Mandie's determination and confidence grew. She
hardly breathed while she waited for the diversion
Tsa'ni would make. She tied Snowball to a bush.

Suddenly the two men jumped to their feet as a
loud noise like falling timber sounded from the woods
behind them. Mandie saw Sallie look quickly in that
direction. Then Tsa'ni's rope sailed through the air
and wrapped itself around the big man, and he struggled to free himself. Just as Tsa'ni had said, the
smaller man ran into the bushes and disappeared.

Mandie ran into the clearing and reached Sallie. She began cutting at the ropes holding her
friend.

"Mandie!" Sallie exclaimed, "Please be careful. The other man may come back."

Tsa'ni came out of the woods and struggled
with the big man and the rope. Uncle Wirt's horse
became excited with the noise and began stomping and snorting loudly.

Mandie was so nervous she had a hard time
holding the knife steady enough to sever the rope.
She had one of Sallie's hands yet to free when
there came a terrible thrashing sound behind her.
She glanced back and saw the big man struggling
with Tsa'ni on the ground. They rolled over and
over.

Sallie snatched the knife from Mandie's shaking hand and finished cutting the rope. She ran to
Wirt's horse and grabbed a rope from the horse's
harness.

"Get back, Mandie!" she called. And Mandie

quickly moved back out of the way. Sallie swung the rope with all her might and managed to capture one of the big man's feet with the loop.

The man began kicking with his other foot and Sallie said to Mandie, "Help me pull this tight." Mandie did what she asked, and Sallie tied the other end of the rope to a small tree trunk. The man continued to kick, but the rope was tight around his foot.

Tsa'ni was strong, but he was only fifteen years old and a lot smaller than the big man. The girls stood watching the two wrestle and tried to think what they could do to help. Suddenly the man pulled a knife out of his belt.

"Tsa'ni, he has a knife!" Sallie yelled. She walked closer, holding out Tsa'ni's knife and yelling, "Here's yours!"

Just as Tsa'ni managed to get a grip on his knife in Sallie's hand, the night air erupted with the sound of what Mandie thought was a thousand horses and a million war whoops. Her blue eyes opened wide in surprise as Uncle Ned, on his horse, galloped into the clearing and jumped down to assist Tsa'ni.

There suddenly seemed to be Indian braves coming out of every bush, and they descended upon the big man. In seconds, Tsa'ni was struggling to his feet as the Cherokee men securely tied up the big stranger, who seemed to be in deep shock at the sight of the group.

Uncle Ned took Sallie in his arms and, for the first time, Mandie saw tears in his eyes as Uncle Ned held his granddaughter close. Tears streamed down Sallie's face as she cried, "My grandfather!"

The old man smoothed Sallie's black hair and

said, "My granddaughter!" He kissed the top of her head.

The old man saw Mandie standing alone and he reached to enclose her in his embrace. "Jim Shaw's Papoose!" he said.

Mandie found herself crying in spite of everything, and she sobbed, "Please forgive me, Uncle Ned. I was the cause of Sallie being kidnapped. We shouldn't ever have left her alone in the cart."

Sallie looked at her friend and explained, "But I did not stay in the cart. When I saw the men coming, I ran away into the woods. I am ashamed to say that I became lost. Late today, the strange men found me down by the creek and captured me."

"But I shouldn't have suggested going up that mountain in the first place," Mandie said. "I'm sorry." Mandie reached out to hug her friend.

Uncle Ned released the girls as a man's voice behind them said, "You have one man tied up now. Do you know where the other one is?"

Mandie looked up to see a tall man with a shiny silver star on his chest and a wide-brimmed hat on his head talking to Uncle Ned. Uncle Ned had brought the federal marshal with him. "When Tsa'ni roped this man, the other one ran away into the bushes," she told the lawman.

"We will find him," the man said. "Let's fan out and search the area. And remember, these men are wanted by the federal government. They are dangerous."

The lawman led the Cherokee men into the underbrush. Mandie and Sallie stayed with two of the braves who remained to guard the big, strange man.

He started mumbling angrily, "I should have hit

you with that arrow that day on the mountain while I had a chance," he yelled at Mandie.

Mandie walked over to stand in front him. "Do you mean to say you are the one who shot arrows at us on that trail?"

The big man replied with a sneer, "That was us, and it's a downright, dirty shame we didn't put you out of commission right then and there."

"And are y'all the ones I've been seeing following us everywhere we've been going?" Mandie asked.

"That's right, we know every move you've made—you and these here Injuns," the big man said.

"Come away from him, Mandie," Sallie urged. "He is not worth talking to." She pulled at Mandie's hand.

Mandie allowed Sallie to lead her across the clearing toward the warmth of the fire.

"Do not waste your breath talking to such people, Mandie," Sallie said. "The lawman will take care of him."

"You are right, Sallie. Now that we've found you—" Mandie suddenly looked around and realized Tsa'ni had disappeared. "Where did Tsa'ni go?"

Sallie also looked around and said, "He probably went with the men to look for the other crook."

"There was so much excitement all of a sudden that I completely forgot about Tsa'ni. He was the one who found you, Sallie," Mandie told her.

"I know," Sallie said. "And I am grateful. I will let him know that."

"I don't remember seeing Dimar or Uncle Wirt in the bunch of men who came with Uncle Ned," Mandie remarked.

"They are possibly with another search party,"

Sallie said as she bent over the fire to warm her hands. "All the men do not go in the same direction when a search is being made."

Mandie suddenly heard a loud meow and she jumped to her feet. "Oh, my goodness! I plumb forgot about Snowball," she said.

At that moment, Tsa'ni came into the clearing holding her white cat in front of him as though he didn't want to touch it. He came straight to her and said, "Here is that silly white cat."

Mandie took Snowball and held him close, "Oh, thank you, Tsa'ni. I forgot to go back and get him."

Tsa'ni didn't answer Mandie, but he looked down at Sallie as she sat on a rock by the fire. "Are you all right?" he asked.

"Yes, thanks to you, Tsa'ni," Sallie replied as she looked up at him.

Mandie noticed scratches on the boy's bare arms and she said, "Why, Tsa'ni, you are hurt!"

Tsa'ni glanced at his arms, gave her an angry look, and said, "I am not hurt. The big man only scratched me."

"Tsa'ni, I really and truly appreciate you letting me come with you to rescue Sallie," Mandie told him.

Tsa'ni didn't even look at Mandie. He glanced at Sallie and said, "If you are all right, I must go now." He quickly vanished through the bushes.

Mandie and Sallie looked at each other.

"He is a strange person," Mandie said. "I never know how to act around him."

"I have always believed Tsa'ni is really shy, but he puts on a big, mean personality so people will not know it," Sallie said.

Mandie looked across the clearing and saw the

Cherokee braves bringing the other strange man into the clearing. The lawman was leading them.

"At last they have captured the other man," Mandie said excitedly.

Uncle Ned came over to the girls and said, "Now. We go home. Now."

The girls were more than ready to go. Uncle Ned had a wagon waiting at the bottom of the mountain and he himself drove them back to a happy Morning Star. Soon the entire community had descended upon Uncle Ned's house in celebration of the safe return of Sallie.

Mandie found Dimar and Riley O'Neal among the crowd. They had stayed with Uncle Wirt who now sat drinking coffee by the warm fire.

Mandie and Sallie washed their faces and hands at the water basin as Riley O'Neal and Dimar came to talk to them.

"I am so happy you are all right," Dimar told Sallie. "We went to the other ridge with Mandie's uncle Wirt to search there."

"It's such a relief to see both you girls are all right," Riley O'Neal told them. Then with a grin he added, "Especially since tomorrow has been declared the first day of school. This is in honor of our safe return."

"The first day of school?" Sallie said in surprise.

"The school is really going to open tomorrow?" Mandie asked.

"Yes," Dimar told Mandie. "And tomorrow night we will have our festival around the fire by the schoolhouse for you to tell us about your European journey."

"Things sure are moving fast all of a sudden," Mandie said with a laugh. "But then they have to, because I will have to be going home in a few days to get ready to go to school myself.''

''That's why we've moved things up,'' Riley told Mandie.

''So I wouldn't have a chance to back out of these things, right?''

''That is correct,'' Dimar said, smiling at her. ''Now that the lawman has taken the imposters away, we will be able to accomplish these things.''

''Imposters?'' Mandie asked.

''Yes, they were impersonating government men, and the federal marshal was after them before they ever showed up around here,'' Dimar explained. ''They were trying to dig up artifacts. Which it is our custom to bury with our dead.''

Mandie's voice saddened. ''Oh, how horrible! I'm so glad they've been taken away.''

Uncle Ned came to where the young people and Riley O'Neal were standing by the back door.

He spoke to Mandie, ''Papoose, we go to Franklin at the second sun-rising from now.''

Mandie knew he meant the day after tomorrow. ''I'll be ready, Uncle Ned,'' she assured him.

The old man took an envelope from his belt and handed it to Mandie, saying, ''From grandmother of Papoose.''

Mandie was surprised that her grandmother would send her a letter with Uncle Ned. But then Uncle Ned had been to Asheville where she lived. She took the envelope and said, ''Thank you.''

Stepping away from her friends, she opened it. There was one sheet of neat writing which read:

Dear Amanda,
    Do not be late returning to school. There are rumors that Hope and Prudence Heathwood

may be selling their school. We want to evalu-
ate any new owners before we decide whether
you should continue attending there.

Love,
Grandmother

"Well!" Mandie said with a sigh. She was so surprised she didn't know what to think. If the school
was sold and her mother didn't want her to continue
there, where would she be sent?

Mandie realized her friends were watching her.
She stepped back over to tell them, "My grandmother says my school may be sold."

"Then you will have a new headmistress," Sallie
said.

"I am not sure my mother will continue sending
me to that school if different people take it over,"
Mandie said.

"Maybe you could come to our school," Riley
O'Neal said with a smile.

Mandie smiled back, shook her head, and said,
"I'm afraid not. It's too far and inconvenient to get
to from home, for one thing!"

"Mary Lou will be coming tomorrow for the
opening of our school," Riley said. "Maybe she
would know of some school that your mother would
approve of."

Mandie looked at him. She remembered seeing
that name signed to a letter in his room. "Mary
Lou?" she asked.

"My sister Mary Lou," Riley explained.

"Your sister," Mandie repeated. *So he has a sister,* she thought.

"At least you may be rid of April Snow if you go

to another school," Sallie told her. "She is always causing so much trouble."

"But my friend Celia Hamilton may be sent somewhere else," Mandie said. "And then there's Aunt Phoebe and her husband, Uncle Cal. If someone else takes over the school, they may fire them."

Dimar said, "Look at the situation this way: There is nothing you can do about it until you return home. So enjoy the rest of your visit here with all of us."

Mandie smiled at the tall, good-looking boy and said, "You are absolutely right. And I do enjoy coming here to visit. Now, we need to discuss what you want me to do at the festival tomorrow night and, Mr. O'Neal, we should talk about the first day of school coming up tomorrow."

Mandie and her friends went to sit on the back stoop to discuss plans. But in the back of her mind, Mandie worried about what was going to happen concerning her school.

Maybe she could talk Miss Hope and Miss Prudence out of selling the school. Maybe she could get up a petition from all the other girls there and persuade the two ladies not to sell.

In fact, she might even get the boys at Mr. Chadwick's School for Boys to help out, since the two schools were often involved in social events together.

Maybe it will all turn out right, she thought.

———————

Many of Morning Star's recipes for Cherokee dishes are in *Mandie's Cookbook*, available at your local Christian bookstore.